"[Richard Chiem's] words have brains that have bodies that wake you up in the way waking can be the best thing, like into a warm room full of good calm remembered things that feel both like relics and new inside the day."

—BLAKE BUTLER, author of
Three Hundred Million and *There Is No Year*

"Richard Chiem captures the mundane depravities of being young and alive with lucidity and a touching, weird grace. Everyone should live in his world for a little while."

—KRISTIN IVERSEN, *NYLON*

"[Richard Chiem]'s swiftly becoming one of our great chroniclers of urban melancholy."   —*ZYZZYVA*

"Richard's stories are as generous as he is. They are the quiet, electric moment between the lightning flash and the thunder rumble. And they have the same odd light."

—MATTHEW SIMMONS, *Hobart*

Praise for *King of Joy*

"This novel is transfixing: an imaginative meditation on emotional survival, isolation, and the beauty and limitations of human connection. I love Chiem's writing."

—MELISSA BRODER, author of *The Pisces*

"What a funny, fresh, bittersweet masterpiece—there is no one else in the world writing like Richard Chiem. From the sentence-level wizardry to the racing plot, I feel smarter just having read this. Every page brings a new set of wonders."

—ALISSA NUTTING, author of *Made for Love*

"*King of Joy* is a perfect rendering of that feeling of dark and hopeful closeness with loss I've always known but could never put to words." —CHELSEA MARTIN, author of *Caca Dolce*

"Richard Chiem writes like someone whispering in your ear. He's insistent and methodical, and you want to hear every word he has to say. *King of Joy* takes Chiem's unparalleled voice and carefully amplifies it, ratcheting the tension until you're not sure where he stops and you begin. It is a brilliant, tender examination of the unholy magnitude of trauma. It shows how pain can simultaneously destroy and preserve a person. Most of all, it is just goddamn beautiful writing."

—KRISTEN ARNETT, author of *Mostly Dead Things*

"In *King of Joy*, Richard Chiem shows us what it is to live in the immediate, day-to-day song of forever grief. Each sentence is masterfully written and equally afflicted by the one craving that affects us all, which is the desire to belong. This book turns pain over and over in its raw mouth, exposing what it is like to feel longing in its deepest, most hidden form, and teaches us more than we could have ever hoped to learn about pure love, loss, and the hard work of accepting the human condition."

—ELLE NASH, author of *Animals Eat Each Other*

"What did I just read? I don't really know, but it was just a little bit mind-bending. Chiem's writing is mesmerizing and perfectly suited to a skipping narrative full of strange and disturbing things (there are porn movie sets and hippos and a very good dog). I can't wait to see what he writes next."

—ANTON BOGOMAZOV,
Politics and Prose, Washington, D.C.

Praise for Richard Chiem

"Considering how much I love Richard Chiem's writing, and given how its uncanny snare and sweep of life's especially agile, prompt, messed, lithe, sharp, and heartbreaking things leaves me stiffed of summarizing words, I think I'll just nominate his work for immortality."

—DENNIS COOPER, author of *The Marbled Swarm*

"Richard Chiem writes of all the weirdness and ooziness and tenderness of young love, with such lucid specificity."

—KATE ZAMBRENO, author of *Book of Mutter* and *Green Girl*

KING OF JOY

ALSO BY RICHARD CHIEM

You Private Person

KING OF JOY

RICHARD CHIEM

SOFT SKULL  NEW YORK

This is a work of fiction. All of the characters, organizations, and events portrayed in this novel are either products of the author's imagination or are used fictitiously.

First Soft Skull edition: 2019

Library of Congress Cataloging-in-Publication Data
Names: Chiem, Richard, 1987– author.
Title: King of joy / Richard Chiem.
Description: First Soft Skull edition. | New York : Soft Skull, 2019.
Identifiers: LCCN 2018040349 | ISBN 9781593763091 (pbk. : alk.
  paper)
Subjects: | GSAFD: Mystery fiction.
Classification: LCC PS3603.H5468 K56 2019 | DDC 813/.6—dc23
LC record available at https://lccn.loc.gov/2018040349

Cover design by salu.io
Book design by Wah-Ming Chang

Published by Soft Skull Press
1140 Broadway, Suite 704
New York, NY 10001
www.softskull.com

Soft Skull titles are distributed to the trade by Publishers Group West
Phone: 866-400-5351

Printed in the United States of America
10 9 8 7 6 5 4 3 2 1

For Frances

I would never rest again: I had stolen the hunting horse of a king of joy. I was now worse than myself!

CLARICE LISPECTOR

PROLOGUE

DEAD MAN

There were months where I did the same things for weeks at a time. Meals were interchangeable, my outfits moved on and off me, and there were days I had no opinion, my mind blank, walking home alone following palm trees overhead. I remember looking around during different parts of the day: leaving the apartment complex, cruising around the grocery store, reading at a bar after work, having a smoke. Everyone was having a different conversation than I was. All the strangers, everyone was moving quickly in and out of the rooms we were in together, anxious to be somewhere in the future. I was watching and imagining I was away from here: I was gone, walking around with Corvus in Paris, going somewhere to be with friends. I don't know why it was always Paris in the rain.

There were months I felt as though I had no head, or I did the same things for long stretches of time, and it became surreal. Days were less and less about anything. People often refused to make eye contact with one another or looked spaced out. I pretended I was indestructible to pass the time, painting house after house or taking whatever odd job I could find, working seven days a week, and sleeping defeated in bed when I was exhausted. I watched wall clocks and digital timers. Sometimes I would change positions in bed to try something else. My foot would be where my head was, and my head where my foot was. I slept every way I could in my sweet bed, creating solitude from malaise.

I would walk in the daylight without wincing, thinking about Corvus. It was my favorite activity, repeating routines, in uniform or in transit, until I would be closer to her. When we were reunited, it felt so good it was as though I had survived some sort of trauma or natural disaster, being away from her. Although there were days I felt nothing, I could go as cold as nature to the awful things around me. I could be quiet in a room and feel alive.

The building could collapse onto me and I would still tell you I needed to get back home to her.

Tape recorder clicks off.

PART ONE

WANTING OBLIVION

CHAPTER 1

IN STORY BOOKS, IN MOVIES, AND IN POP SONGS, CORVUS has always loved the stubborn characters the most: the grim warrior fighting impaled with a sword in her abdomen; the lost dog running from state line to state line to get back home to her owner; the loser getting kicked in the teeth and choosing to smile, mouth full of blood, instead. Still, having not eaten all day, Corvus thinks, What am I doing here? There's a fucking tree on fire and no one is doing shit.

Outside, half-naked girls are popping open champagne bottles, shooting corks high into the trees and screaming into the night air. They laugh and run in circles around the trees. Clouds of hot breath. Minutes earlier, the one with blond hair approached a tree with a burning torch and, unblinking, set the leaves on the lowest branch ablaze, feeling the heat against her face as the tree caught fire. Everything is foggy and dark except for the burning tree and the girls dancing in the shaking light of the falling cedar.

Corvus lights a cigarette. She smiles at how scary it is here and laughs at herself. But she has always loved proving a point, that nothing will ever kill her. Nothing kills me, she thinks.

The phone rings and trembles on an oak table in the middle of the large room, an old library on the third floor of the house, as Corvus looks out the window, watching the other girls dance. She blows smoke against the glass, leaning arms crossed against a cold pillar. Tim is the only one who ever calls this line, she remembers.

Corvus answers, Hey. She gives the impression she's been through this routine before although she's new here.

Tim says, I need you downstairs in about five minutes, okay?

She says, Why do I know your carpet?

What?

The carpet in here, the library. I know this carpet from somewhere.

Tim says, I should have fucking never brought you here.

What? she says.

The carpet is everywhere in the house, right?

Corvus nods but doesn't say anything. She takes another drag with no face.

Tim asks, Have you ever seen the movie *The Shining*? The carpet under your feet, and everywhere in the house, is exactly like the carpet in *The Shining*.

•

Grief is an out-of-body thing, the worst secret you can have. You live in one terrible place trapped inside your head while your body lives in another terrible place entirely. Corvus is tired in a way that feels like there's no going back; like everything from this point on will be brand-new, full of things she has never seen before, moments she has never wanted before. It's like when you're finally eating after a long day of not eating and not knowing how close you were to killing someone or collapsing from how starving you were. She can feel it in her bones: there is no going back.

When she lost everything, she had Tim's phone number to call; he offered her a way out of the hole. She wouldn't have to think about money, she wouldn't have to think if she didn't want to think, he said. She could just disappear into the woods, he said. Make a movie. Get drunk, get high. Make money far away from the evil city. There is magic and healing in the woods, he said.

The pay phone in the middle of the tall grass is ringing, causing all the women to turn their heads in unison to look and stare for a moment. Corvus holds the phone to her ear and watches the reflection of the empty library behind her, a spinning ceiling fan and rows and rows of hardcover books, before she returns her focus to the movements outside. As horrible as things are, she can always sing a song quietly to herself. She loves songs about real love and tragedy: the best pop songs ever are sad songs.

Another tree catches fire from embers in the wind. Some

of the girls are in the grass, six or seven of them, some others are running deeper into the dark woods. Some are screaming, Money, money, money! We are going to get paid!

The blond girl runs over to answer the pay phone, her bare feet trampling the tall yellow grass as she makes her way through. She knows exactly where to look toward the house, finding the window as she picks up the phone.

Even from this distance, Corvus feels a small chill of fear when they suddenly lock eyes, and the blond smiles with the torch still burning in her other hand.

She answers, Hello, this is Amber.

Corvus says, Hey.

What are you doing?

Corvus says, Not burning a tree. What are you doing?

You should come down here and have some fun with us.

Corvus asks, Why is there a pay phone out in the middle of nowhere?

Tim likes the phone here. This isn't the middle of nowhere, don't say that. Amber says, I don't know, I think it's really fun.

The burning tree finally falls down and shakes the earth but Amber doesn't look away from Corvus. Amber keeps her hand on the phone and waves the torch in a dead way. She says, Please come down here.

Corvus says, The burning tree fell down. Why did you start that fire?

Amber drops the torch from her hand and it stays lit on the spare gravel around the pay phone. As though meditating, the girl never breaks her stare, secretly digging her toes into the little rocks and pebbles, undisturbed by the cold. Although she can't quite see it, Corvus can feel Amber's face change from one thing to another. It starts to rain then pour. Freezing tiny droplets fill the giant window.

She says, Corvus. Please, come down here.

Three days earlier, Corvus walks through baggage claim aimlessly, still feeling the ghost of the airplane vibrating all around her. Airports secretly thrill her, she feels as though she is somehow closer to death or another realm here, walking in slowness from escalator to escalator. She has a favorite sweater with her, one she wears when she's really depressed or behaving strangely, because it makes her feel like no one could fuck with her, a long wool sweater that reaches her knees, with soft hanging sleeves and a big collar.

There is a boy outside arrivals and departures waiting for his ride who offers Corvus a cigarette. He lights it for her while she sits on her suitcase, staring at her reflection in his sunglasses. There is some reckless abandon there and a calm face. She smiles and says she's new to California and he says, You're a natural already.

Easing her tensed neck against his shoulder, Corvus watches a plane disappear behind clouds and readies her body for anything. She has the makings to detach herself, to endure pain with nonchalance, drifting almost to sleep, jet-lagged with this new stranger. His ride is a Jeep with a driver who looks exactly like him, and they look so uncannily alike it briefly scares

Corvus. She has found twins. They offer her a ride to the house in the woods where Tim is waiting.

Impulse begetting impulse, she looks at her phone and decides to let Tim wait a little longer before she enters her new life. On the highway, her heart races with suggestion, and for the first time in over a year there is no one she wants to call, there is no one in the world she wants to see or talk to. Suddenly, she wants to do all the brand-new things. Anticipation is so much better than real life, she thinks, and I need a drink. Corvus breathes as though she's swimming, taking in small pockets of air and holding her breath at the same time, her hair flying everywhere in the backseat of the fast Jeep. She wants something outside of her body.

Corvus asks the twins, Hey, what are you doing right now? Can we do a detour? I would love a detour.

They take her to a nice hotel, leading her into a small room, their hands on the small of her back. She says what she wants, leaning back for leverage. They both come at the same time and Corvus watches the miserable expressions on their faces, finally not identical at all. When they ask her to stay, the two of them naked together on the bed, she says, I can't. I really can't. I'm here for business, not pleasure, but thank you, boys, that was nice, and she leaves the moment, walking down the narrow hallway, not looking back, as though she owns every floor in the building, as though she can move all the elevators in the building with her mind. All her limbs are stronger now and everything is brighter.

Alone, waiting for the elevator, her body aches with the

slightest memory of being pulled apart. It is a little past four in the morning. The smallest things take courage and weirdness and sometimes complete blind effort, she thinks.

Corvus enters the hotel kitchen, steals a muffin off a white plate on the counter, and leaves through the back door, gently shutting the latch behind her. Outside, she looks for the main road with the address to Tim's house in the woods memorized by heart. In the surveillance tapes, Corvus walks with a muffin in her mouth, a bloodied sweater tied around her waist. She drips unknowingly behind her as the camera turns. She shivers like no one would ever know.

Corvus answers the phone still vibrating in her hand, discovering a dozen missed calls. She quickly glances at the screen before saying hello.

The voice says, You weren't at the airport.

Corvus says, I know. But I'm here now. I want the job, she says, feeling something like pain somewhere on her body, but it's not quite pain.

There are scratching noises outside the door, the light pulsing underneath. Corvus washes her face with her hands and smiles for a breath before holding the door ajar. For a moment, she doesn't see anything, only the same narrow hallway and weird carpet. There are paintings of a single landscape repeated along the entire length of the wall, what looks to be simple rising ocean waves and jagged rocks and a girl standing out at the edge of a cliff. The sound is a drone coming from outside, the muffled screaming of disembodied happy girls. For a second Corvus almost forgets she isn't alone here.

Then, at the end of the hallway, she sees a pack of brown pit bulls treading in rhythm, each lively and muscular, heading for the stairs. One immediately senses Corvus, and runs back down, jumping in the air to her open door. It slams mindlessly against the hinges, crashing into her right side. Corvus leans down, using the door like a shield. She spends a few minutes convincing herself that her hand is not broken, shaking her hand in sharp pain.

Corvus opens the door right as the dog charges again. This time the animal stops, doesn't pounce, and looks up at Corvus, who's bleeding from her hand. Whatever movement she makes she makes without breathing. The dog has lipstick prints all over his face, all different shades and colors, panting in place with his entire muscle of a body. She holds her hand out. The dog comes over and licks the cut on Corvus's hand, whimpering as she comes down low to him on the ground. He whimpers like a puppy. Corvus says, Good boy. Good boy. I love you already.

She walks downstairs.

Her eyes grow accustomed to the dark and she can see figures emerging in the room. The dog is no longer panting by her side, but Corvus can faintly hear him banging against walls and yelping somewhere in the house. The pit bull is a little space she owns in the dark, a small truth she uses to calm down, something to focus on and follow around in her mind. Listening to the sound of a door opening with no door to be seen, and with no light to be found, she almost wants to say something.

Struggling to see, Corvus clenches her fists, bites her lips, and waits for what's next, breathing so slowly she feels a slight euphoria. Nothing changes for a few minutes: no movements, the large dark ahead remains, every fiber of sound seems imagined while she inhabits herself not moving in place. Corvus crouches to the floor, consciously cracking her knees. She says, There is no place I would rather be.

Lights flicker on in the basement, a dim then suddenly bright room coming alive. Her eyes can finally see everything. All the girls from outside dancing in the woods are here, ashy from the fire. Some are smiling, some are expressionless and stoned, lined up touching hip to hip only a few feet away from her. Corvus can see empty porn sets being lit up behind them, almost every one filled with clouds of balloons or stale rose petals. Everything is clean and soft and motionless.

Tim comes walking in through double doors with a camera and tripod in hand, shaking the floorboards, and says, It's time to clock in.

Amber steps out from the row, the first of the women to be so bold, and says, Don't be scared.

She takes a long time to walk over to Corvus and pets her hand, held inside her own. Her aureoles are small and tan like the rest of her body; her pulse is the softest, warmest ticking. Corvus still hasn't seen Amber blink once since they first made eye contact, before she suddenly winks at her.

They lean into each other and whisper back and forth.

Tim sets up his camera, lighting a cigarette as he aligns the viewfinder with the floating balloons. Some of the girls wave at him but he stares straight ahead to the backdrops, smoking his cigarette, watching it burn.

After a moment, Corvus nods and steps forward, a blank face. She takes off her shirt and starts to lightly stretch, her shoulder blades rotating like a dancer warming up. Under her breath she says, I fear there is no such thing as being naked.

There is porn and there is porn and then there is Tim's method of living with his actors. He claims great success and high Web traffic and that's why the direct deposits are so large and steady, he says. He preaches high art. I'm always with you, so I know you, I know how to film you, he says. He says this and repeats it like a signature calling card to all the women on set: It's because I'm always with you, baby. People are watching. Money, money, money!

Sex becomes entering a room and leaving a room, pounding heartbeats on a schedule. Sex becomes muscle memory. After a few days, Corvus begins to find a rhythm in her new life. Her body surprises her, her mind continues to drift endlessly, and by each day's end she can hardly describe the way she feels. It is quite possible she feels nothing.

After settling in, as in her other life, Corvus keeps to herself. What is there for her to talk about anyway? She says, I don't mind being alone here. The women watch her, and she watches them. Her eyes glaze over. She wears a black ski mask, once a favored prop, casually around the large house in the woods. In her black ski mask, Corvus watches the forest from her balcony as though something is about to arrive, as though something is going to pop out of the woods. She is happy just to feel like she doesn't want to die.

Corvus starts with solo videos before working with other women. The other women start requesting to be with her. When Tim is in the scene, Amber is the director. In truth, Amber is a gentler cinematographer, her shots look like photographs, focusing on faces and fingers and soft hands.

The very first time with Tim, he doesn't say much. He starts undressing, gives Amber a thumbs-up, and stares at Corvus as though he is speechless. Taking his time, the buttons take forever.

Corvus looks up at Tim from the bed.

Tim says, I'm not Perry.

Corvus at first says nothing. Her face turns white and she loses feeling in parts of her legs, grabbing hold of the headboard. Shut the fuck up, she says. Shut up. Hurry up.

Amber fires a gun of confetti in the air, the red light of the camera blinks low battery.

Corvus uses every single breath in her lungs for timing, not making a noise, and for a moment she thinks, hiding safely inside her head, that some things are easy. As easy as falling. Some things she can do.

CHAPTER 2

A YEAR LATER, WOOZY WITH INSOMNIA, CORVUS WAKES UP feeling as though she has been living the same day inside the same week inside a dull year, repeated over and over again. Strange routines pace her invisible life. Pornography bores her, but she loves the smell of the giant redwoods and the quiet of the trees. An enormous moon lights the empty patio. She watches the night sky from the kitchen. She hasn't seen a bird fly by this place in days, and then she finally sees one in the moonlight: she can't tell what kind of bird it is, but she watches it until it disappears out of view.

Corvus walks barefoot and yawns. The poise and happiness of her years are gone but she owns a slowness no one could take from her, a rock no one could dare budge, drinking cold chocolate milk straight from the carton, more in her head than anywhere else. The house pipes hum beneath her without her having a sense of them. The lie she tells sometimes is that she's doing okay, that there is nothing wrong. Most days, there is nothing to say.

Feeling something larger than belonging to people, something alone and masterful, Corvus makes fists with her toes, clenching her legs and buttocks, as she reaches for the ceiling. Memories blur, soft pain diminishes. Corvus watches the beginning of sunlight glowing in the trees, looks at the garden appearing outside the window. She says, I miss you, baby. She wonders if prayer can somehow exist in all manners of time, an invisible guardian angel who can always relay messages, so he would always be able to know how much she loved him.

It takes a few moments before Corvus hears someone else's breathing, and she turns to see Amber sitting on the stairs, half-naked, legs crossed under her oversized Slayer T-shirt.

Amber asks, You don't like the light on? Do you mind if I turn the light on?

Corvus says, I don't mind. Whatever you want.

Amber walks closer to Corvus without turning any lights on, sighing on her way over. She rubs Corvus's neck and looks out to the overgrown gardens. She stands behind her and runs a single finger down her spine.

She asks, Are you hungry, Corvus, honey?

Corvus barely nods and says, I could be.

The garage door trembles as it rolls up flat to the ceiling. Getting into the passenger seat, Corvus unlocks the door for Amber and tilts her seat back. Amber scoots inside, slamming the door, and touches Corvus's inner thigh. Sunlight creeps in, and the radio turns on with the ignition, a sad pop song.

Pebbles shoot up underneath the hood, creating nothing, small vibrations.

Seat belt.

Corvus says, Seat belt.

You know, I've never listened to much Slayer, Amber says. Or any Slayer. I don't know why I love this shirt so much.

Corvus asks, Never?

Amber shakes her head, slowly accelerating downhill through the wooded pines to the highway, the only car on the road in all directions for miles. For some reason, Corvus imagines elk running alongside the highway with the high speed of the car, racks and heads lowered and tucked down. The trees are being so quickly passed, it's as if they flicker.

And then she sees one real elk, only a single one and he's standing by himself, already a great distance behind them near a steel traffic barrier. The elk appears so large for so few seconds. His head tilts up with the wind, his antlers scratching against the bark of a tree, shaking the branches.

Amber says, I don't know why I lie about it.

For a long stretch of decline after the woods, there are still no other cars, except for a single sixteen-wheeler speeding past them, quickly exiting off the narrow ramp, softly rattling its big chains and cargo. Corvus imagines the cargo under the black tarp, from caged chickens to empty pipes to chemical tanks, unable to stop inventing. She can daydream whole days and live transported. Together Corvus and Amber listen to the DJ talk about death row groupies and the change in global climate before Fleetwood Mac comes on, "Never Going Back Again."

Corvus asks, Was I talking out loud?

Amber puckers her lips and shakes her head. No. I didn't hear anything.

Suddenly Amber is wearing sunglasses. The sun is rising.

There are no photographs in the house, only paintings and mirrors and plain brown wallpaper. Tim likes to collect video, and the only televisions in the house are all in his editing studio. The sky above the house today is so blue you can almost hold it, but no light comes through Tim's side of the house. No windows.

Tim knows it is a special day and he feels a thrill, a little kick in his step. He makes sure no one is behind him and walks lightly on his feet through the hidden door behind his closet, behind his hanging jackets.

In his studio, all of the TVs are turned to mute, a sea of quiet movements. Most of the TVs play pornography on a loop. An entire wall of light and pornography. All of the hundreds and hundreds of VHS tapes on racks along the wall are labeled with clean white stickers.

Tim walks over to the rack and pulls out a tape.

White label, black letters: MOMMY.

He pushes the tape inside one of the VCR players and all the screens suddenly sync to the same black-and-white image: a woman in a rocking chair in front of a fireplace. She's facing away from the camera and looking at the fire. Tim remembers as a child loving to record the fireplace and watching the flames for hours. He can hear his mother silently nodding her head, rocking expressionlessly in her chair. The lights in the house were always kept dimmed or turned off. She hated everything the light touched. Like clockwork, she struck Tim senseless in the sunlight.

Living under her roof for thirteen years in mostly dark rooms and hallways, Tim molded a quiet person to grow into. He's even quiet when, on screen, his mother clutches her neck with a stiff hand in sudden reflex and collapses like a sack of bricks to the floor: a stroke. Tim remembers not responding. He remembers no panic, no out-of-body travel. He didn't try to resuscitate her, search for help, or even walk closer. Tim had instead walked over to the home entertainment center and played a VHS, *The Shining*. He had walked downstairs to the kitchen and made two Hot Pockets and watched the microwave until the timer beeped.

On the wall of TV screens, his mother shakes before she stops moving, and she's contorted herself almost off camera. The body stops moving, and the fire burns in the background.

Tim remembers picking up the camcorder, walking it closer to his mother so it looked right down at her. He had turned the camcorder around, and now all the screens show Tim's young face. He has just turned thirteen, and there are crumbs on his chin.

Tim turns up the volume. Little Tim says, Mommy is dead. All the screens say, Mommy is dead. His voice is distant and warbled but his face on screen looks relieved. His eyes look happy.

Tim rewinds the footage and starts it from the beginning. He watches it over and over again on the wall of televisions. Today is the anniversary of her death and Tim celebrates with cheap red wine, Klonopin, and Hot Pockets. He is King Klonopin.

Look at you, Mommy, he says, all by himself. He slurs his words.

Tim walks to a cell phone ringing on his desk. The ID reads PARTNER, the phone vibrating in his hand.

Tim answers, looking for a cigarette, and says, I was thinking about painting again.

Something is muffled on the other end. He powers on his monitor and searches his website, checks his bank account, accesses sister sites and more pornography. The blue screen reflects in a square inside his glasses; the pupils are large, dreamy, and dilated. The top three requests in red font on a black background:

Teen (399)

Abuse (543)

Snuff (1674)

Tim asks, How is the hippopotamus? The hippopotami.

Her mood changes when she is finally sitting down at the diner, Amber scooting in next to her on the same side of the red vinyl booth. Corvus stares through the window at the spare traffic, feeling somewhat frail then comfortable before some despair seeps in, a brief dark moment when she's not blinking or moving, not really looking at anything at all. There is no song in her head today. But for a moment, there is no stress. Nothing better to focus on than the window and the highway, the way the overcast is breaking up in the sky.

Amber admires all of Corvus's faces and follows her line of sight. Beyond them like paintings are endless cedars and the almost pitch-dark forest, and more trucks are creeping for open parking spots outside the diner. Sunlight reflects off the parked cars and the wet pavement, and the diner's morning rush is gorgeous: tall muscular men dressed in flannel and jeans or business suits. Corvus quietly accumulates thoughts and deep inner strength, taking large sips of coffee, keeping her chest warm. She craves a cigarette.

The long tree branches sway in waves in the wind. There is an element of fear in how slowly Corvus is breathing, as she watches the rustling forest. Bright yellow and red leaves fall to the ground.

Amber takes a bite of her pancake, chews despondently, and says, If only disappointment burned more calories.

Corvus says, If only.

Amber says, Some days, I don't want to wake up in the morning.

Corvus says, I've been having trouble sleeping. But I'm used to it.

Through the window, a single cyclist rolls uphill and past the diner. A sparrow, just above him, flies the other way.

The men inside the diner barely say a word. Chew, chew.

The conversation from booth to booth, table to table, is muffled and far away. Sleepy, nothing conversations. Corvus takes a moment and wonders where everyone is going today, ignoring her faint reflection in the window, eyes glazing deeper out. Another cyclist passes.

Amber says, Hey. I almost forgot. Amber licks and sucks the maple syrup from her fingers and reaches in her purse for something. She takes out and lights a small striped blue candle and sticks it through a muffin top. The blueberry bleeds a little. The music on the loud stereos in the diner is another pop song. The candle burns and glows, and Amber grows ecstatic and softer, even easier to be around. She says, Happy anniversary.

Corvus says nothing and stares at the candle.

Amber says, I can't believe it's been one year since I've met you.

Corvus blows out the candle and says, Thank you for being so nice to me.

A snap, a sound in the distance: a loud barking. A fuzzy brown spot bounces along the edge of the road. It vibrates and grows bigger and bigger, running out of the thick of the forest and heading to their exact window at the diner. The girls rise in their seats, each pressed against the glass, suddenly alive with a rush of adrenaline and a feeling of phenomena, something like peaceful alignment. Empty of incoming traffic and pedestrians, the road looks as though it can go in both directions forever, everything surrounded by hills or trees. The pit bull jumps up and down at their window, barking happily, and Corvus immediately recognizes the dog. Her heart pounds in recognition. Amber covers her face in glee and jumps up and down in the booth as though the dead could walk and are walking right now, and the men in the diner all stare at them, some smiling and some tapping into cold, cold looks.

Amber says, Oh my goodness, he followed us here!

Amber's eyes are all pupil.

Corvus says, I love this fucking dog.

Everyone has their favorite particular body part, Amber says, walking barefoot from the cool stone marble balcony, her soft robe billowing around her in the draft as she comes into the main room. She says, I like collarbones, veiny hands, and I like feet, too. And shoulder blades. Everyone should always appreciate a good shoulder blade.

Corvus lies on the floor in her sweater and says nothing, one leg bent to the ceiling, carefully watching the glass chandelier above her. She realizes she doesn't know what she wants or where she needs to be. She doesn't know what to do with her days here, and she's not really sure what happens now or what happens next. Mindlessness is next to godliness, Corvus thinks, and although she feels a little anxious, there is little fear in her. It feels good to go with the flow without a plan. Gone are the days when she felt perfectly at home. Corvus plays a secret game of holding her breath, a deep breath, and not moving a muscle. Uncertainty is fine.

The pit bull lies down next to her, flopping and resting his heavy head on her stomach.

Amber stares at her feet on the hardwood and says, I haven't worn shoes in days. She wiggles her toes like her feet are thinking.

Corvus exhales and says, I like collarbones too, and nods without looking at Amber or the other girls in the room, who are popping Klonopin like icy breath mints. All of them are either sprawled out like Corvus on the floor or playing pool a few yards away. She can hear the snap collisions of the billiard balls, the echo of the hollow pockets every now and then being struck. Looking straight up, Corvus watches as Amber slowly appears, upside down and standing over her, her blond hair almost masking her face, a shadow blocking the light from the ceiling.

Amber says, I like your collarbone, and walks to the pool table, touching the small of everyone's back on her way there. Her way is enchanted, Amber's magnetism tickles, and the room responds to her in smiles and warm laughter. Small tattoos, birthmarks, and little scars cover nearly every naked body. While admiring their beauty, Corvus thinks about literally pouring herself out, every last drop. She likes that one stupid song of being bled dry.

The music playing downstairs suddenly shuts off and all the girls look up startled as though staring at a trapped bird in the room. They glance at the intercom speakers. The quiet turns to reverb before the air clears again and there is the sound of Tim clearing his throat, a dozen throats in unison in one dozen speakers all over the house. He clears his throat again.

Tim says, Night shift. Five minutes.

Amber leans on the pool table, closes one eye to focus, and sinks two balls with one strike. Smiling, she says, Come on, ladies. Time to make that dollar.

Even the dog rises.

The speakers vibrate again: Five minutes.

All the girls walk in pairs from one end of the living room to the narrow wooden stairs at the end of the hallway, Amber walking ahead of them in the dark, playing a ukulele, entranced in a song. Suddenly she is singing and her singing is breathtaking and the women follow her. Amber sings, *Songs keep coming even happy to be sad*, and her body relaxes into the faint echo of her voice. The girls murmur and yawn, rank and file, holding wineglasses and water bottles. Nice little cocktails. Everyone is here for a reason and that reason is to get a little bit more destroyed.

It's never as easy as it seems, walking from point A to the next, Corvus thinks. Something shifts and aches. Corvus looks at her hands before she, too, gets up and walks over, following the pack, lighting her last cigarette, alone in the bright room. It feels so good to walk. She drifts in and out, past and present vistas, quietly transported. The pit bull follows her but stops before the stairs and whimpers at the threshold of the door as though approaching deep, deep water. He looks measurably freaked out.

She asks, What's wrong, baby?

Corvus can see Tim at the bottom of the stairs, only part of his face visible in the light.

The pit bull keeps crying and clenching and looking down.

Corvus says, The dog is afraid of you.

Tim looks sideways at something and says, He's a smart dog.

Looking up at her, Tim says, Fear is healthy.

Corvus breathes and exhales smoke, feeling wide awake.

Do you have another one of those?

Corvus says, No, it's my last one, and she gently tugs the dog's ears and walks two steps at a time down toward Tim. Her pace is eager, and the smoke rises. The dog, head lowered, whimpers shrill cries even after she leaves earshot, moving her body closer and closer toward the bright stupid confetti. He keeps watching her before she disappears in black and white. Although he is brave, there is not enough dog in the dog to move him past the threshold. His legs can't move but he can wait for her. It can be five minutes, an hour, weeks, or forever, and he can still stand there, be a sentinel, and wait for her.

Corvus drinks icy white wine to cool her warm face and watches Tim mumble something under his breath as he makes the bed, fluffing the silk pillows and checking to see if he likes the mood lighting through the viewfinder. The camera hums in his hands. The set is the same as yesterday: tripod, red velvet curtains surrounding the bed, a forgotten broom tucked away in an off-camera corner. Everything seems poised to get better.

She tilts her head back and wants something. The torture Corvus feels on most days is certain but at least she has an active inner life, she thinks. She manages peace and quiet in her contemplation, dependent on absolutely no one but herself to create the worlds in her mind. The beach, the woods. The blue house in the city, in the valley, on the farm where she will never live. She is never alone because she is always alone, her private koan, her rock within a rock.

In the light, Corvus yawns and pops her ears, out of focus on the screen of the camera.

Tim walks closer to the girls but doesn't say anything. He looks into a handheld camera and mumbles incoherently. Corvus can hear him now. Tim says, I am searching for beauty. It is happening right now.

She notices how soft his voice is.

Amber approaches on Rollerblades. The noise, the grinding screech of the wheels on the hardwood, is comforting. Tim walks over and kisses Amber on the back of her neck, kisses her hair, and says, Go to the bed.

Looking at the fallen confetti and pillow feathers spread all over the polished furniture, the rows of empty beds, Corvus feels her heart contract a little with fear. This seems different. It seems special, the way everything is arranged. The set is much cleaner than Corvus has ever seen it, and it's as though Tim is being more careful. There are bottles of champagne set in bowls of ice all around the room. There is powder on Tim's nose and fingertips. He is sharing his entire stock for the shoot tonight and says, Enjoy the pharmacy.

Worry moves through Corvus. She almost says, Amber.

All the other girls flatten against the wall, most of them topless or fully nude, except for Corvus in her sweater, again the one black sheep in the group. The ringing in her ears is gone and she can hear clearly now.

Spread like a star flat on her back on the bedding, Amber has no tan lines, the life behind her eyes drug-coated and miles and miles away. The ceiling is one grandiose painting of lush clouds.

Tim starts recording and begins undressing. There is something handsome in his hostility, the tension in his shoulders, a twisted, charming thing he does that Corvus can identify. He makes you want to know why he's angry and he never gives an inch. Her face is still warm. Tim announces he has a new cock ring.

He clenches his hand into a hard fist and starts smacking Amber in the face, rapidly punching her cheeks and nose. The metal bedsprings squeak with each smack, and Corvus screams with no sound, her blood on fire. The sounds grow wet, like slabs of meat falling to the ground. Corvus covers her mouth with her hands before she sprints over, making out Amber's quiet moans, the sounds her skin and bones make. The other women, all drugged out of their minds, look at one another, more confused than afraid. Some hold hands; some rub their gums and their teeth. The lights stay bright.

Tim senses Corvus behind him and quickly jumps off the bed, walking with a deadpan look on his face into the camera's line of vision before shutting it off. He looks into Corvus's eyes and says, It's unbelievable how things can dovetail, so fast and so bad.

Corvus almost says something, but a hard breath in her lungs makes her pause, before Tim's head knocks violently forward, his eyelids fluttering. He falls to the floor and, behind him, Amber continues hitting him with the dull end of a broomstick, all over his body with no discretion. Amber takes a moment, looks at Tim lying there on the ground, and drips and says, I can take a beating, and starts beating him again. Corvus can hear two things: the broom and flesh. The broom handle is made of solid gold.

A timer releases bright confetti from the ceiling, synced right at the storyboard's predicted climax. It comes like clockwork, raining in every color Corvus could ever want to see.

Corvus repeats softly, I can take a beating.

It seems like many moments, the length of time it takes going from dream to dream, before Amber walks over, breathing heavily, and says, Let's go. We should go.

Amber says, Let's go find our tapes first.

Corvus remembers and says, Our tapes.

The room is a mess. The other girls look around the bloodied basement in awe as though everything has changed, because everything has. Some of the girls are getting up, running their hands through their hair, silent witnesses. Corvus jogs up the stairs, her wrist held by Amber, and looks down on everything and everyone else. She tells herself she needs to be present. She needs to be here. She looks at Tim lying facedown on the ground in a small pool of blood and waves to the girls staring up at her. There is a scratch in her throat, a black hole. Corvus whispers, The future is right now.

•

There isn't a chance in the world. Corvus wants a sense of peace, like touching something warm to get warmer, but the feeling doesn't come, and they keep driving away. The sky clouds over in dark storms, the engine hums and vibrates. In the backseat, the pit bull sighs, resting his head on his legs. He is a dog with presence, with big lungs. Corvus stares out the car window, experiencing a small sinew of longing, and turns silently to Amber. Some of her hair in the wind gets caught in her mouth.

There is blood on Amber's face; the house in the rearview mirror is shrinking smaller and smaller out of sight. Little by little, they make a pact with knowing glances, sharing strange sorrow twisted in a secret with each other: they need to be gone. They need to get the fuck out of here.

The flowers on either side of the highway, all native to the region, are changing colors, from lavender to sunflower. The deer and elk sleep in the dark. Corvus wants a wolf or something else lonely to howl or scream but nothing answers. No wind outside the car.

Amber says, That's funny.

Corvus asks, What?

My foot is asleep. Amber says, It's tingling.

CHAPTER 3

EVEN WITH ALL THE ANGER THAT BUILDS, CORVUS HAS THIS small hope that she can survive anything, see everything through, endure and take on the days as they come. At ten years old Corvus already knows the world is a scary place. Full of sick, twisted people. She knows to cross the street when a strange figure appears ahead, keeping her hands in her pockets, never looking meek or afraid. She crosses dry streams and paved streets every day. Corvus watches the leaves on tree branches shake in the wind and avoids eye contact with everyone; her eyes gloss over people. She loves how wet things get in the fall, how the sky is reflected everywhere, watching planes fly through puddles, disappearing in the pavement.

On the walk home from school, on the other side of a chain-link fence, Corvus can see a man masturbating in a brick alleyway with another man watching. The other man is smoking something. They both wave at her and smile from far away. She can feel them waving and smiling at the corner of her eye as she treads uphill toward home. Inside her head, not paying attention to the road or the trees, Corvus likes that they both looked happy back there. She runs the last few blocks home, her book bag bouncing, her hood falling back.

Finding her keys in the threshold, she thinks about how she loves coming home, how coming home is one of her favorite things. Slamming a screen door feels like perfect. She hangs her jacket and finds her cigarettes, hidden inside her owl piggy bank, a pack of Newports and a pack of Reds. The sunlight fades from room to room, dust bunnies float along the ceiling beams, and Corvus watches shadows while making hot ramen on the stove.

She loves the house empty and to herself. Her father is always working or at the casino, her mother runs her secret errands and sometimes never comes back home at all, for nights on end. No questions, though. Her mother leaves no contact number to call but sometimes a twenty-dollar bill.

The wind hits the side of the house that leaks and rattles. Corvus cracks an egg and watches the yolk, golden in the broth, tilting her head back as she smokes. She mouths a sad pop song. Her prized possession is an alarm clock radio that she never turns off, and a broadcast is always playing somewhere in the house.

Corvus blows smoke into the spinning ceiling fan and calls her friend Michelle, who lives just down the street and around the corner. She bites her lip when Michelle appears on the front porch dressed in short shorts and a baseball cap. Michelle is two years older and already developing. Hugging each other near the vines, they share a cigarette before walking out back to the swimming pool; leaves float in clouds on the surface of the water, the last rays of light trace the edge of the pool.

The water laps. They dip their feet, sitting close and watching geese form flocks on the horizon. Corvus feels like dying a little.

Corvus says, Hi.

Michelle smiles and says, Hi.

Did you bring it?

Michelle nods and brings her bag around, unzipping it and showing Corvus an unlabeled videotape. It's heavy when she holds it.

Corvus asks, From your dad's again?

Michelle says, I watched it earlier. There are three guys in this one and the girl kind of looks like you.

Really?

Michelle nods and says, Really.

Corvus finishes the last of the cigarette and gets up to throw the stub away. She says, Goodbye, geese, and stares into the sun, no hand in her face.

Corvus hugs Michelle from behind. She says, Come on, no one's home. Let's go upstairs and watch it.

CHAPTER 4

AFTER HOURS OF DRIVING IN THE DARK, AS THOUGH OUT OF nowhere, there is a bright neon motel sign and a diner emerging from the hill. A wide smile on a hot dog painted on the side of a red brick building makes Corvus feel demented, realizing she aches for a shower and a warm place to lie down. Her eyes feel new and different as though she has just woken up. The dashboard clock glows blue in the dark: 3:22 a.m.

She can hear a helicopter and a single car, maybe highway patrol, pass by the motel parking lot and Corvus feels reassured by the quiet that follows. There's still a faint smell of blood and wet dog in the car. Corvus watches the rain, illuminated under a nearby streetlamp, before she can make out Amber walking out of the manager's office and opening her driver side door. Corvus blows on the cold window. She writes *HELLO* on the foggy glass and draws a happy face as the other door slams.

Amber says, Let's go, I got us a room.

Corvus finds Amber in the reflection, not turning her head around, a little lost in thought. Completely still. Push and scream.

In the window, Amber says, HBO. HBO. She pumps her clenched fist.

They unlock the door and walk toward the bed like zombies, not bothering to turn on the lights. Corvus falls facedown on the comforter, her backpack falling to the floor, and Amber goes straight to the bathroom. Corvus nearly falls asleep before she hears the shower going, the sounds of steam and light water splashing; she can hear a soft wind from outside the cheap wallpapered walls. Although she has an urge to go check the blinds, she stays right where she is, sinking into the little give of the bedding. For Corvus, the bed is a small lake where she floats and keeps her face still, the only movements are from her chest as she breathes, from the rare long blinks she makes to the low ceiling.

Amber walks out of the bathroom in her robe, drying her hair with a towel, and puckers her lips. She is all clean, all smiles, and she looks good in this light, Corvus thinks. Steam climbs to the ceiling, the bathroom fan humming.

Corvus almost violently sits up, flailing in the bed, and says, Oh, fuck.

What? Amber asks. What?

Corvus quickly rises, her hair disheveled, and goes for the door. She says, We left the fucking dog in the car.

She opens the door and rain blows in, wet leaves all over the carpet.

•

Pink oleanders melt into the pink sky at dawn. Their limbs feel frail and smooth. The motel room seems bigger somehow and lush and vibrant. Corvus realizes this is the longest she has been sober in more than a year. She remembers eyeing Amber back at the house in the woods for the first time and seeing her friend Michelle in Amber's eyebrows, in the way Amber leans in doorways, the way she laughs before nodding yes to things. Corvus sees herself at age twelve walking to Michelle's house, watching Michelle laugh on her patio, walking with Michelle toward the deep woods, sometimes scared of the woods, sometimes feeling completely free.

Amber laughs and nods, and says, Yeah, I guess I do that.

The light hits her face and collarbone; she's a known quantity.

Amber laughs with her whole body, leaning backwards and arching her back on her tiptoes if she finds something really funny and it has her completely.

Where is she now? Amber asks. Michelle? What happened to her?

Corvus says, She died a couple of years ago.

Amber sits on the floor, wrapped in her robe, and makes a nice lap for the dog, and says, I'm sorry. I'm really sorry. She pats her lap and baby-talks to the dog. The big boy comes over, wagging his tail. She says, I love that dogs are better at reading body language than humans are. Human body language.

There is something distant and sorrowful in how little her

head moves when she's talking or listening to other people, Corvus thinks, how her gaze stays fixed on various inanimate objects in the room. Eye contact can be this sweet torture. Corvus remembers Michelle doing the same thing: they would spend hours talking and staring at chandeliers and window blinds and not looking at each other. The air conditioner clicks on, hums, and, without placing why, Corvus feels compelled to be here.

Amber reaches for her bag, and her robe droops a little open. She starts rolling a spliff; the dog doesn't move. He snorts and lies down in a heavy thud. She takes a drag and leans against the wall, close to the radiator, smoke circulating through her mouth and nostrils. She inhales and blows smoke rings.

Amber says, I miss you, baby.

What?

I heard you talking to yourself once, one night in the kitchen. It was the same night we went to the diner, remember?

Corvus asks, And that's what I said?

Yeah. Yeah, that's what you said.

Amber gets up to hand Corvus the spliff and offers her other hand. Do you want to talk about anything, Corvus? Did you hear what I said? Amber asks, Who were you talking about? Who were you missing?

Sitting at a desk, Corvus stares at a cheap painting of blue waves crashing against a lighthouse and holds a matchbook. She fidgets and turns it by its four corners like a square wheel. When Corvus finally looks back at her, Amber doesn't dare say anything. It's as though Corvus is still waiting for something else to happen, as though she is trying to summon something from outside her mind. A thought passes slowly from beneath one still eyeball to the other still eyeball, a cold chill. Amber almost expects a knock on the door.

Corvus says, He died a couple of years ago too.

The rubber seal makes a sucking sound as Amber pulls open the refrigerator door and, for a moment, it does this thing and takes over her mind. A moment of peace flurries, puffing cold air, a nothing noise. A cloud in her face. She whispers, Shut the fuck up. Amber peeks her head inside and pulls out an unexpected bottle of champagne. Someone left this here, she says. She wiggles the bottle and dips her shoulders, dancing. Her hips, too. She apologizes for being stoned, her first of many apologies for being stoned, smiling and showing gums.

Amber's face is a little bruised, some slight swelling shows on her cheekbones, but she's less damaged than Corvus imagined she would be after what Tim did to her. At any part of your life, a slightly out of the ordinary shock is all it takes to unnerve you from your everyday genius, Corvus thinks, the comfort gets sucked out of your routine like air in a vacuum, the core where your courage comes from grows cold and isolated in an instant, not quite useless, not quite present. Corvus studies the details and little things. Amber has a high tolerance for pain and her untouched peace of mind seems to be as though from another place, from a whole new scary way to relate to someone.

Corvus asks, Are you scared? About Tim?

Amber takes a drag, puckers her lips, and shakes her head no. I would rather talk about you right now. She uncorks the champagne and licks the overflowing fizz with a smile. The sounds of hip-hop from the small radio dull her senses, the beats and bass waterfalling in repetition. The drugs fog the foreground.

We can talk about whatever you want to talk about, or not talk about, I don't care, sweetheart.

Corvus says, I don't feel like moving.

We can just talk.

The dog lies on his side, his legs dead to the world. His tail whips sometimes from deep REM sleep.

Corvus smiles and says, This is strong. She pinches the last of the burning roach and leans her head back. Dying embers disappear. Smoke and sweet aroma. Amber watches from the dark, the only light in the room is the television, which takes a long time to come into full picture.

Amber puts in a videotape marked CORVUS.

Corvus says, I really hated my whole life before I met Perry. My husband, his name was Perry. And I could, I could feel what he meant to me, our bizarre connection, almost right, right when I met him.

Amber stares at the paused Corvus on the TV screen, an image from just a couple of years ago, a static white line like a lightning bolt staggers across her face, and without turning her head around, Amber says, Go ahead, honey. I'm listening, I'm listening.

CHAPTER 5

I keep everything that horrifies me a secret. I pretend that everyone around me is having the worst day of their life. These are etiquettes I practice to weave in and out of the world. I wait in lines in public and lament my past lives. To the woman standing next to me at the bus stop, the lonely cashier at the food co-op, the crowd on the street that pours around me: I imagine you're having the absolute worst day and I won't mess with you. I won't add to your day. I see everyone with the sun in their eyes and I look back at them.

Corvus stretches out in the hallway. She's wearing a new black dress under my sweater that's hers, lying on the floor, full body stretch. The dress is off the shoulder, the floor is wall-to-wall carpet. I have been away and we have been apart and because we are hard, sad people, I feel fragile when I come into the room. *Seeing Corvus brings me immediately home, our inner lives come to life. We shut the blinds. Smoke. Fuck. Smoke. Drink. Fuck. Smoke. Perfect cartwheels in bed. Champagne and serial television.*

My usual anger: it opens like a flower and evaporates and vacates. Corvus reaches for me and we go to our desired stupor.

She says, Fuck me numb. The day keeps tearing at me.

With words half in me, I can't quite trace my steps once I get home, and I leave my mind with Corvus. I still wonder. I keep going. I keep going, I keep going.

She whispers in my ear, I admire the way you whittle. All the way down.

Tape recorder clicks off.

DEAD BLACK ELMS ARE PILED ON THE OTHER SIDE OF THE construction site. The few yards on the other side of the chainlink fence used to be forest and old growth and it's now bleakass shit, torn-down trees, blocks of concrete, and dug-up earth ruptured for another parking garage, soon to be the tallest one in the city. Corvus keeps a wad of paper in her jacket pocket and walks through the excavated grounds, weaving through the giant equipment, ducking through the hole in the fence underneath the NO TRESPASSING sign. She scratches her back on the fence, ignoring the slight sting from the wet steel. Grimacing, she crushes wads of paper until they're nothing in her pocket. Her bad habit, if she has to name one, is twisting the fabric of whatever she's wearing tightly inside her clenched fists when some shit has gone down. She remembers telling

Michelle, When shit goes down and I feel this pressure, I don't even notice that I do it. I just start crushing things in my hands.

When Corvus can't sleep in the middle of the night, she likes to sneak out of the house and walk to her high school, feeling like a fourteen-year-old loser, seeking comfort in empty classrooms and hallways. She likes the acoustics of being alone at school. Having no other place to escape to, the quiet feels more quiet. No one bothers her here.

Her insomnia is worse during the full moon, which Corvus watches in the sky as she makes her way up the school steps. The door, close to the gym, has an old bent lock, and Corvus lowers her shoulders and pushes hard through. It makes a loud clunk sound and then nothing, everything's okay. She walks a couple of laps in the hallways close to the gym lockers, having a desire to run away from home forever, before she hears something.

Following a not too distant cry, Corvus runs down the hallway, pink in the face. She can see all the stars through the big glass windows and her mind is quiet. The school walls give off a comforting chill, an almost hum. The little, tiny sound Corvus hears is a meow—she is almost certain—and she tries to pinpoint where it is coming from. She runs past all her normal classrooms: AP History, Advanced Chemistry, Sad Rooms Forever. Walls of lockers and trophy cases and bulletin boards.

A calico kitten with a white face is trapped inside a vending machine, her spotted paws tapping the inside of the glass, its jaw opening wider and wider with each cry. The kitten is trapped behind the HH latch, the salted pretzels. Corvus runs over so quickly she drops her bag, unaware of her hand covering her mouth. She says, Poor furry baby! Her hand on the other side of the glass, shadowing the paw.

She presses HH and unzips her book bag.

Walking the stone path home through the cemetery, she knows most of the names engraved here by heart. She likes some gravestones more than others, she likes some of the names more than others, and she has her favorites. She imagines the lives of all the names here when she gets the chance to be alone and away from everything.

Corvus whispers, Kitty, I wanted to die today but instead I took a walk. I took a walk and kept walking for a long time and then I got a little lost, I think. I read all these gravestones. She kisses the cat's ears while the thing purrs. Corvus yawns and shakes from the cold in the glow of the moon; her breath puffs visibly in the air. She says, Let's run away together. Corvus meows and says, You and me. Let's run away together, Kitty.

Corvus gasps, I fucking can't. She says, I fucking can't, barely getting any air. Her first ever panic attack. Her legs are paper.

With some of her belly exposed, flat on her back on the floor, Michelle reads from a thick textbook: *The brain keeps developing and developing and thus forming throughout an entire lifespan*. Michelle looks up from the page, snaps the book closed, and says, So you're a new person all the time.

Petting the cat, conscious only of her own little world, it takes a soft moment before Corvus sees Michelle is staring. She smiles and says, The word *develops* makes me think of breasts. The brain develops like boobs for an entire lifespan.

Michelle cackles and pedals her feet, fondling her own breasts in mime, and the kitten torpedoes out the door for no good reason. The door rattles and a little draft comes through. The girls laugh and shiver in unison, tears swelling in their eyes as they come down from their high.

Corvus looks where the door is ajar and says, I have a bad feeling about the kitty. I feel like something really bad is going to happen to the kitty.

Michelle takes another hit from the pipe and in a haze says, It's kind of scary but I was feeling the exact same way. She looks toward the hallway as though something were creeping by on the other side of the wall. She says, Like that cat is totally going to die.

On her forearm, Corvus sometimes writes phrases she likes or something from the day. Tonight, the words are *burnt childhood photos.*

Michelle takes another hit, holds in her breath, and her eyes water more. She moves her mouth like a goldfish, talking while trying to hold her breath. She asks, So, are you coming to my party?

Corvus says, You know what I always say. No cute boys, no party.

Yeah, you suck, Michelle says. You never come to my parties.

I don't want to come because people suck. High school kids suck, Corvus says, smiling.

Michelle catches a glance of Corvus's forearm and reads what it says. She says, I didn't see any baby pictures of you downstairs.

Corvus makes the words heavier with a black pen and answers, My mom burned them when she was hammered one night. There's not one left.

She almost carves her arm with ink.

Michelle watches carefully, holding her breath, as Corvus deepens her tattoo. There's even a little blood.

There are moments Corvus can feel a shift happening. Where does all the good go? Michelle flicks her cigarette into heavy rain, waves goodbye, and leaves through the back door. Corvus can hear her mom's rusty truck pulling into the garage, and the engine dies; the headlights illuminate the carpet hairs from beneath the door, then black. Without knowing what possesses her to do so, Corvus quickly rushes to turn off all the lights and hides behind the curtains; her hurried breathing brings her pulse pounding to her ears. When she tries to calm herself down, she says, There is no center, there is no center, over and over again. There is no center ever.

Her drenched mother stumbles in the front door with a strong wind, and little things flutter in the house, magazine pages and opened letters. A gigantic man almost twice her mother's size follows her in. He shuts the door gently behind him and whispers something into her ear. She says, No, laughing. My daughter is asleep, and James is at the casino.

She shakes her hips, swaying backwards, and hoarsevoiced says, I'm all yours.

Keep your body still, the man says, locking the door behind him, and he touches the light switch.

He says, The lights are off. They take swigs from the flask chained to his belt.

Corvus paces her breathing from the dark shadow of the curtain. She stands there like she is never leaving the curtain, like she has become part of the house, like she is changed forever. She watches her mother and the giant embrace and kiss before racing each other for the bedroom upstairs. Listening to their footsteps, it dawns on Corvus anew how horrible her mother is, how this keeps shocking her enough to care. Their moans fill the house, sounds bleeding through the thin walls, and Corvus remains stiff among the curtains.

When she finally leaves the curtains, she walks to the everplaying radio in her room right at the moment the phone rings. Just past midnight. My Bloody Valentine. The kitten looks dead asleep in the space between her bed and the wall. The phone reads, PAPA.

Corvus answers, When are you coming home?

What? His voice is warbled.

Corvus can hear slot machines in the background. A little louder she says, When are you coming home? You haven't even left the lobby.

He takes his time, taking a drag from his cigarette, and watches anonymous women drift across the room, a sea of lights, bells, and chimes.

Corvus says, Papa.

I lost another ten thousand, he says. His breaths are tense and measured.

He says, I think this time I'm going to die, I'm so stressed out, baby. Papa doesn't know what to do. I don't know what to do, I don't know what to do.

Black markets. Hired killers. Orca whales. Idle times, little moments to herself, can drift her mind to strange, comforting places. Imagined worlds and perfect self-movies. If only Corvus could be an actor playing herself in a movie, she thinks. Perhaps then things would become more manageable: the terrain would be known, life all-encompassing would be her choosing, her challenging role to play. It would all be just a game, for real. Everything would be easier, death would end the movie.

Corvus, after hanging up the phone call with her father, lets the air eat at her from all over. There is a ringing in her ears, a buzzing on her skin. Fuck, she says. Fuck me.

Without packing a bag, she runs out the back door to Michelle's house. The door slams. The rain is freezing but running down the middle of the road feels transformative. She feels more alive, more present; the air has a charge. The rain behind Corvus seems to be falling from all directions, endless droplets bouncing high from the dark pavement and parked cars.

Michelle answers the door immediately. She can't see Corvus's eyes, can't tell if she's happy or sad, crying or drenched.

I thought you said you weren't coming to the party, says Michelle. Something fragile in her shakes from the breeze and the pleasant surprise. Just having Corvus there in front of her has always silently delighted Michelle, and she smiles in flashes every time Corvus makes her way back to her. Corvus is breathing hard, her face hidden inside her black hood. There is a mouth there.

Smiling to her gums, Michelle says, You said, No cute boys, no party.

Corvus asks, Can I ask a huge favor?

Of course.

Corvus asks, Can I bum a cigarette?

Michelle reaches for her back pockets, opens the door wider, and fishes for her lighter. The music, vibrating the walls inside, is hypnotic, so melodic. Boys in baseball caps and polo shirts walk up and down the hallway, girls in baseball caps and high-top sneakers sit and smoke on the steps. Michelle hands Corvus her last cigarette. She asks, Are you crying?

No, Corvus says, shaking her head. It's raining.

Someone hands Corvus a Polaroid—it's a photo of herself she doesn't recognize—and the boy who gives it to her is the chubbiest at the party. The photo feels like a gift from a nightmare, something she should not be holding. It's scary to see you made it through a night you don't remember. The feeling is like eyeing a speeding car rush past you, missing you by an inch or a second. There is a ringing in her ears still, her face bright and damp. Outside, the rain slackens, and trees push against the windows of the tall Victorian house.

He's the quietest boy at the party but he's polite, Corvus can tell that he's polite. He waits with his head down and doesn't say anything; he hands her a red plastic cup of water.

It is a Polaroid of her biting a knife with an unknown hand cupping her breast outside her tank top. In the photo, her eyes are closed, and she looks more at peace than she has been recently.

She feels a tingling on her neck and the turbulence of the dryer in its final spin against her back. She's wearing Michelle's old Slayer T-shirt, which is stretched at the chest, waiting for her clothes to dry in a nook by the stairs away from the party. A small birthmark on her chest shows above her camisole underneath: it looks like a crescent moon. Corvus likes this boy almost immediately and she arches her back, watching where he stares.

She imagines having larger breasts than she does. Corvus says, Thank you. I don't remember this. She shakes the Polaroid like it's developing.

He looks up at her and sticks out his hand and says, Perry, my name is Perry. That's my hand.

It is, says her voice.

No, I mean that's my hand in the photo.

She says, This is you?

Corvus looks at the photo again and looks at his hand and says, I don't remember this at all, Perry. She doesn't reach to shake his hand.

Perry appears shocked to hear his own name. His face glows, and he stands a little straighter.

Perry nods and says, I'm sorry, I think you were really drunk. And sad about something but you wouldn't say. You stuck out a knife toward me and asked me to take a picture. You yelled for my hand.

Corvus whispers, Jesus. I'm sorry.

Perry hands her a joint and says, No, I'm sorry, and walks away to the other end of the party, into the cloud of smoke and dim neon. The dance floor lights up downstairs. Corvus watches Perry join the others, a sea of dark bobbing heads, young bodies.

A bedroom door is flung open and Michelle walks out, her skirt rolled to her waist. There is blood on her knuckles as she smiles and walks up to Corvus. Michelle says, Hey.

A boy with a bloody nose runs out of the room looking upset, holding his baseball cap in one hand. He nearly falls on his face scrambling away.

Michelle sits next to Corvus on the stairs and Corvus can see Michelle's clothes are nearly ruined, there are little tears here and there. Michelle says, I lost a button.

Corvus asks, What happened to that guy? She eyes a small trail of blood on the carpet.

Asshole kept telling me to smile so I told him to smile, says Michelle, her voice sounding hollow and far away. Michelle takes the Polaroid from Corvus's grip. She asks, Did you say hi to Perry?

Did you see this happen?

Michelle starts cackling, leaning her head against Corvus's chest and collarbone.

Michelle says, You don't remember? The other night. You pulled a knife on that guy and ordered him around. It was funny as shit.

Corvus asks, What else happened?

You did another shot of tequila and told him you liked him a lot. Michelle's eyes look as though she is about to faint. She says, You told him to get you high the next time you see him.

As quickly as she came, before Corvus can say another word, Michelle leaves and follows a new boy in a baseball cap down the hallway. She can hear Michelle say she's lost a button, repeating herself over and over. Corvus catches herself mouthing song lyrics, looking dreamily into the dark mass downstairs, the throbbing hip-hop. Her mind fires and fires, forming his face as it was just now.

In the dark smoke, Corvus approaches Perry and touches the small of his back and says, Hey. She whispers something else in his ear but he can't quite hear what she's saying; the mob of bodies around them swarm and bump and grind. The bass speaker vibrates the floor and the skin of bare feet. Some faces are kissing. Corvus says, I'm sorry for pulling a knife on you.

Perry moves a strand of hair around her ear and says, It's okay. His face is expressionless, blue like the hovering neon light above him, then green, then purple.

She asks, Were you scared?

Perry shakes his head and smiles at her. He says, I'm not scared of you.

Corvus says, very clearly, You don't have a baseball cap.

He says, No.

Touching his chest, Corvus says, I really love that. Corvus holds the joint between them and asks, Do you want to go somewhere?

Her heart pumps new blood as she leads him with their fingers interlocked out the back door and away from the pounding stereo. A little calm arrives with what little terror she feels. The crowd parts. On either side of them: gossip and bodies, red cups of jungle juice, perfume and body spray, bright young faces. Perry seems like he's there to listen to her. He is easy to be around, the hand in the picture, this brand-new person. It goes quiet between them. She feels her pocket for a lighter before he slips one into her hand and gently curls her fingers around it. In the wet woods, a fog settles around them. They can smell mint in the air.

Her mother is talking to herself again, sitting at the edge of her bed, empty bottles of Navy-strength gin in rows at both ankles. Corvus glides by the crack of her mother's open door and slips into her own bedroom at the end of the hallway, knowing where in the floor doesn't creak.

Stripping off everything, she doesn't breathe until she's under the covers, pretending to sleep. The night catches up to her and she aches in parts, as though her body is expanding. Hugging her knees on her side, Corvus finally falls asleep, a fog of a dream creeping from one end of her mind to the other, a dead blank expression from ear to ear, a little drool drop.

Everything from head to toe tingles in deep sleep, ever-moving delta waves. Her mouth open against the pillow.

Corvus dreams an hour-long nightmare in seconds, a frenzied figure keeps following and chasing her, and she cannot seem to get away, running up and down hallways she doesn't recognize. Whoever is following her is always right where she turns her head to look. Because she has never met him before, in her dream the man chasing her has no face but a large, always looming body.

A sudden creaking outside her door signals to Corvus that her mother is there. The sound wakes her, but she does not stir. The kitten under the bed meows at the hallway light just once. After nothing happens, she purrs.

Her mother sits on the corner of the bed and reaches to touch Corvus's hair.

Her mother says, I know you're awake, honey, and keeps caressing Corvus's forehead, running her fingers back and forth through the strands of hair.

I know you're awake.

Corvus feels exhausted from the long party and the heavy rain, and she pretends to be asleep, timing her breaths and relaxing her muscles, listening carefully. It feels important right then to be cautious.

Her mother says, You shouldn't talk to yourself. People start talking about you if you talk to yourself.

Her mother says, I wish you were better. Why can't you be a good girl and not—not a little fucking slut.

She gets up, a power drill in one hand, and the bed rises

with her weight. Corvus's mother leaves the room and presses the trigger, turning the drill on and off as she walks, the mechanical whirring never changing in volume no matter where she is in the house. Corvus cringes and tightens her body. There is a cold that never leaves the house and the chill lingers from basement to attic, room to room. By the morning, every door in the house is off its hinges, some have fallen on the carpet, some are sticking out of the frame as though jabbing out of the wall. It looks like no one lives here.

She wakes with a large blood clot in one eye, her left eye. Because all the doors are gone, the kitten runs laps through the house, sometimes crashing into Corvus's legs. What gauge measures terror, the sudden urge to kill yourself? Corvus wonders. What is the threshold? What are the limits? All of her father's possessions appear to be gone, even his ashtrays are missing.

With her socks on and pillow marks on her face, Corvus walks around her father's office, her bed comforter wrapped around her shoulders like a shawl. His only suitcase is gone and his electronic safe beneath the window has been cleaned out with its door left open. Daylight through the trees cuts the room in half and her face in two.

Plastic and wire clothes hangers scatter the floor of the master bedroom. Corvus's father's closet looks quickly ransacked, only a few old T-shirts left on their hooks, loose ties on the floor. The room means very little to Corvus. She looks around for a note or signs of struggle before giving up and walking to the kitchen. Lying down on the cold tile, Corvus presses her fist against her forehead and imagines digging it deep inside.

Corvus drops her hand and just lies there, absorbing the softest vibrations from the refrigerator clicking on and off, and doing nothing but staring at the ceiling fan. The neighbors are vacuuming again. She lies for hours, skipping school for the day and ignoring the kitchen phone when it rings, lost in her thoughts and dead layers. After being awake and motionless there for hours, Corvus suddenly falls asleep for a few minutes.

Her mother unlocks the front door, the only door left in the house, arriving home from work to see a body on the floor in the kitchen. She taps her daughter in the rib cage with her boot. She taps then kicks. Corvus gasps awake, holds her side, and rises.

Her mother asks, Did you go to school?

Papa's gone. Papa didn't come home.

She grimaces and again says, Did you go to school?

No, says Corvus. Did you hear me? Papa didn't come home. His stuff is gone.

Her mother takes off one of her black steel-toe boots and hits Corvus over the head with it. When Corvus cowers and runs down the hallway, she takes off her other boot and throws both after Corvus. She screams, You always go to school! Always, fuck! You always go to school.

Corvus does not cry. In her bedroom, she slides against the wall, fists a little clenched, wishing so badly she had a door. She longs to slam a door but it feels good to be hated. Nearly out of breath, she reaches to the floor for a pen and writes on her arm: *It's good to be hated.* She says softly, It's good to be hated, willing the walls to catch fire with her mind.

No longer quite herself, Corvus looks around her bedroom as though trying to figure out what the room could be hiding, what futures could be blooming here. The room has a sense of doom about it and she can't seem to find a comfortable way to sit on the floor. Getting on all fours, she looks under the bed for her kitty, clicks her tongue, and stands up to make the signal: a finger-snap. She hears a meow, and the kitty materializes from underneath the bed purring and, in a beat, jumps into Corvus's open jacket. She zips up and kisses the top of the kitty's head, and the kitty in turn looks up, makes eye contact, and purrs again.

Corvus whispers, You're a good girl, and dims the lights. She dips through the kitchen and out the back door, not running until her feet touch the lawn, and then she completely bolts. Sometimes she feels like she is somewhere else, running at the speed of someone supernatural, mapping a private world within the one existing at will. Her superpower: she can check in and out, she comes and goes as she pleases. It's a button she can push her whole life, a handle in a speeding car she can grab on to during turbulent rides.

When anyone asks what she is thinking, Corvus usually answers, Nothing, I'm not thinking about anything. But the truth is she is casually overcome, sledgehammered with dream worlds. Her daydreams are scenes from fantasy novels, sad rock songs, action-adventure movies. She imagines her body in other time zones and places, and she taps in all the time. Right now, though, she has nothing and she is nowhere. Tonight, Corvus feels utterly defeated, she feels ugly—whatever magic she could usually escape to, whatever perfect world she could build, she can no longer feel it. Her stomach feels empty, and she has no one to turn to, no hand to hold, no gold to keep. She can't think herself to somewhere new.

After an hour of running, Corvus reaches a gas station in a part of town she's never seen before. She has no bag or money; she walks slowly to the curb to sit down. The kitty sleeps inside her jacket, warming Corvus from her stomach to her neck. The lights are bright, the smooth concrete lot is wide and empty. Corvus leans against the wall underneath an ad for all-beef hot dogs and pulls her jacket over her knees. Her limbs and skin and nerves are exhausted, her eyes surveil the surrounding yards. But at the edge of the light, suddenly there appears to be someone walking and crossing the street.

Perry stands alone like a man in a dream. He gently walks in between the gas pumps and sprints the rest of the way. Perry sits down right next to Corvus and they match drowsy stares and smiles. Seeing him now does not startle her or make her anxious yet Corvus shakes, smiling with what she cannot convey. The feeling is a big beautiful horror.

Perry says, Hey.

Hey. Surprised.

He asks, Are you cold?

Corvus says, No, I just yawned. I always shake when I

yawn. She regains her small loss of composure. She looks at him and asks, What are you doing here?

Perry points out into the dark, past the highway. Corvus shivers and squints and sees lit windows, the upstairs to a large house on a hill. Perry notices her shaking and takes off his sweater and throws it in her lap.

Corvus touches the material and says, Thank you.

Perry says, You can have it.

Do you live there?

Perry says, I'm visiting, remember? It's my uncle's place.

He says, I looked over from my window and knew it was you. It was the strangest thing. Perry mimes a double take, looking back and forth from where he came from to where he is.

Corvus doesn't look up or down and pets the sleeping kitty in her jacket.

There is some bond between them, an invisible string. The secret lodged inside her that keeps her closed off from other people is lodged inside Perry, too. She can sense this. They beat themselves up in the same way and feel despair just as quickly as the other. More adjusted to the light, Corvus's vision seems blurrier now in a soft haze she likes.

A little winded, Perry leans in and asks, Are you okay? Do you want to be alone?

Corvus nods. I'm just hungry.

He runs inside the Food Mart and she can hear muffled small talk, the chime from a register. Corvus looks up; Perry hands her an ice cream popsicle: strawberry shortcake. They sit quietly and wait for dawn together, silhouetted against the stone wall of the gas station, uninterrupted by a single passing car. The stars surround the dead yellow moon. There is almost no wind in the dry air around them. The crickets sing ad infinitum.

Corvus says, I'm happy I saw you again.

She raises her ice cream a little and says, These are my favorites.

He raises his eyebrows.

Perry says, I had a feeling.

Corvus says, No.

What?

No, I don't want to be alone, says Corvus.

CHAPTER 6

BIG CLEAN AMPS CROWD THE BACKGROUND OF THE SCREEN, electric guitars stacked on top like books. On the tape, Corvus takes a moment to turn her head back and contemplate them. She looks into the camera and asks, Do you play? I've never seen you. Smoke creeps into the shot from beyond the eye of the camera. Tim's voice is clear as a bell and he says, I tried. Not anymore, though.

There is a couch that folds out into a bed, and Corvus thinks about the simple magic in the world. The video recorder sits on a tripod, which sits on a bearskin rug, its mouth wide open. The bear's eyes draw Corvus's attention for a few moments, and she feels a chill on her arms.

Tim presses a button and Corvus can see the camera's red indicator light turn on, and, without thinking, she smiles. She even feels a little thrill. Corvus senses a strange heat on her chest, expecting to breathe in and undress on camera, and she reaches playfully for the buttons on her blouse.

Can you talk about what you're most afraid of? Tim's voice is steady and practiced. The camera focuses in and out on Corvus's face, blurry then clean and clear.

Corvus asks, Excuse me?

Can you talk about what you're most afraid of?

Corvus says nothing.

That's all this is, the video. Tim thumbs behind him to the camera. He says, This isn't a traditional audition, don't worry.

Corvus asks, Excuse me?

Tim looks up at Corvus and waits. I said, Don't worry, says Tim's voice.

Sternly, she says, Sure.

Corvus touches her face and says, You know, Tim. You haven't changed. You're still an asshole.

Just answer the question, Corvus. Fucking shoot me in the face.

Okay, okay, she says. Corvus pulls her hair back and closes her eyelids as though submerged. She says, Give me a minute. She reaches for a cigarette.

The screen turns snowy before becoming clear again. Corvus fades into the picture with her hair down, wearing a different outfit than before: a blue floral summer dress. Her birthmark shows. There is still cigarette smoke in the static shot.

Not being able to control anything, says Corvus. Not having any control.

In addition to videotaping the audition, Tim has also placed a tape recorder on the coffee table close to her. She watches the wheels of the tape recorder turn. A small, intimate sound chirps from the device with each spin.

Go on, he says.

You can prepare for anything. It doesn't matter. You're just as close to death as everyone else, Corvus says. I could never feel a hundred percent happy.

She looks at Tim, not the camera.

She says, Even if things were perfect. There would be this.

This what?

Corvus shakes her head and unclenches her hands and exhales. I would just never feel settled. I knew anything could happen. I had the perfect life, and then— Corvus stops talking. She keeps shaking her head.

I should have enjoyed more, says her voice. Felt less anxious. Perry was perfect.

Tim says, Perry *was* perfect.

Is that Perry's old tape recorder? The one from his plays?

The video flickers and skips, and the VCR vibrates on the glass TV stand.

I don't know, says Tim. Why? Do you recognize it?

This whole thing is sick, says Corvus.

Amber has these gold handcuffs shimmering in her purse, which she shows the camera and the imagined audience on

the other side, shaking the bag's contents. Tim barely registers her being there; he seems serenely distracted with an inner
world. He gestures for her to sit down and stops smiling. The
shot shows Amber looking at Tim hesitantly as he pulls out a
chair. She looks as though she's leaning away from an eerily
tilting floor, as though Tim is a sinkhole. The dark lighting of
the room eats her eyes. He says, Come, come. The metal chair
scratches the tile and Tim turns on a standing lamp.

Amber sits down and winks into the camera before dropping her purse and lighting a spliff she pulls out from behind
her ear. Her eyes don't roll but flicker before going calm in
their sockets. She leans back in her chair and looks dazed. On
screen, Amber's skin holds a soft glow, a subtle but noticeable
outline. Although she sees a sweating glass of ice water, Amber
doesn't take a drink.

Right away, Tim says, What are you most afraid of? The
video quality flickers, turning the image into a river of pixels
and colors. The white lines on the snowy picture remind Amber of nails on a chalkboard, someone crazy needlessly playing
the violin.

Sitting on the motel bed, Corvus and Amber take a moment to look at each other before Tim's face appears beneath
the static on the screen. They both grimace and scoot closer to
see better. The small TV takes over the entire room, the light
enveloping their faces, the queen-size bed, the cheap paintings hung on dull walls. Their eyes look dead and milky and
faraway.

Tim's face fades to Amber's. The video has been cheaply

edited; there is no score or closed captioning. Onscreen, it takes Amber a second to process Tim's words before her eyes briefly fill with despair. She asks, Are you serious? What is this?

Amber looks around playfully.

I'm serious, Tim says. He touches his chest with his fingers. What are you most afraid of?

Corvus pauses the tape and taps the screen. Smug asshole.

Amber massages her foot on the bed and stares at the TV. She says, He *was*. I never quite saw it until now. Why the fuck did he do that?

Voyeur, says Corvus. He's a voyeur. She shakes her head *no* as though tapping into a memory. He's always been one, she says.

Always? How far did you guys go back?

A few years. I knew Tim in college. Or right after college, actually, the year I was married.

Both realizing how tired they are, Corvus and Amber slowly take a look at Tim's paused face. Amber has her mouth a little open and says, I never knew that.

It wasn't important, Corvus says. I'm sorry I never said anything about it to you. Corvus gets up from the bed. She opens a window and the morning sky comes in. Perfect crisp moving air. She says, We stayed up all night.

Sensing something old and tender in her voice, Amber leans on the bed and asks, Do you want to get some breakfast? Or do you want to finish?

Corvus turns around with the sky behind her. She says, Let's finish the tape. Do you care? I don't care.

I don't care.

I don't care either, says Corvus.

Tim lets the phone ring in the other room with a dead serious look on his face. It rings for a long time and fades into silence. Amber listens to the wind batter all the sides of the building and rethinks the question. There are times when she just wants to hear nothing instead of answering a question. How sweet it would be to simply turn everything off. However, trusting her instincts, she commits a little abandon, ignores the pull of the camera, and talks freely without worry, which Corvus and Amber can now both see clearly on-screen.

I'm not really afraid of anything, Amber says. She looks at ease, like nothing in the world bothers her. Looking around the room and twinkling her fingers, she says, I don't know, I feel in control. I live life without fear.

In the gleam of her eye, she has that quiet, hidden something, the ability to soothe or unsettle anyone around her, and she uses it. Call it being erratic or manipulative or call it being disciplined and tapped in, she looks calm as the sea.

Again, the screen goes fuzzy before tracking clear again and Amber reappears. She blinks a few times and takes a few seconds. She still looks calm, shaking her head, like *no regrets, though. Not a one.*

Childhood is the fucking saddest thing, says Amber. She motions her hands, canceling something in the air. I just thought of something.

I used to watch my sister growing up, Amber says, my older sister, Valerie. I used to watch her marvel at things. Little things, like big clouds, tall buildings, bodies of water, a stranger's accent—it could be anything, Valerie loved to marvel. And she was kind. It was so beautiful to watch her consider the world and its weird people. Valerie seemed to welcome all things, anyone, any creature, with open arms. She was almost thoughtless in that way.

Only three years older than me, my sister raised me. What parents? Fuck parents. Mom was gone, Dad was in and out. Valerie was my protector, my buffer to all the things kids shouldn't know about as kids. She dealt with Dad, she found ways to keep me fed, she played with me and always comforted me and told me I was smart and kept me company. All I wanted sometimes was some company.

But I started to notice things about Valerie, as we went from middle school to high school, the same way you notice how one of your siblings is getting fatter or skinnier over the years, except Valerie was getting sadder, less expressive, and less interested in the beauty around her. It was as though she volunteered to become an adult before she was ready, and something was sucked away from her, and suddenly she could be sad at any moment without ever knowing why. But she did it all. For me she did.

I think of Valerie when I think about fear, says Amber's trembling voice. I don't have any. Valerie put me on her back and so now I don't dare fear a thing. She is with me always.

Wait a minute, Tim says, where is Valerie now?

Valerie is dead, Tim. She's dead, says Amber.

Wait a minute. Tim knocks his knuckles against his fore-head. You don't have a sister, he says. You have four brothers, I remember. I remember now.

I've never seen you this worked up, she says.

Tim cocks his head, cracking his neck.

Amber looks into the camera and her cheeks inflate with deranged laughter, her eyes losing any touch of fear. Amber cackles and cackles and she throws a pair of normal handcuffs at Tim, hidden underneath her pressed thighs this whole time. He catches them, befuddled.

Handcuffs, too, are for the gullible, baby. You're too easy.

Get the fuck out, Tim screams. Get out! Get the fuck out now!

Amber runs with her head ducked down as though the roof were about to cave in, giggling her whole way out of the room, unable to help herself. The tape cuts to black, the VCR hums, and the TV shows a blue screen.

Holding the remote control and lying on her stomach on the bed, Corvus says, Get the fuck out!

Amber cackles on her back, legs paddling the air. Yeah, she says. Yeah, I did.

You don't have a sister named Valerie?

I'm the oldest of five, says Amber. All brothers. I raised those little fuckers.

Corvus throws her pillow at Amber's face. The sound of the pillow's impact is startling, louder than expected.

Suddenly, the dog howls in a volume that raises Amber's

and Corvus's neck hairs. They both hop over to the dog, immediately petting his neck, patting his back. He wakes up trembling and looks back and forth between Corvus and Amber.

Poor baby, says Corvus. I completely forgot he was even here.

Amber says, I remember now. He gets night terrors.

Corvus says, I can't believe I forgot about him.

Amber says, I want to be a dog.

The dog howls and howls inconsolably before silencing on a dime, looking up at the blinking girls, as though realizing everything is going to be okay. He is awake.

Motel employees, a few maids and a clerk, crowd the door, no one brave enough to knock and investigate. Faint shadows underneath the door, they shuffle past. The dog has finally stopped howling in any case.

CHAPTER 7

FEELING SUN-KISSED AND SICK AND ACHY, CORVUS FINISHES her champagne in the shower and reaches for the shampoo. The glass fills with water, which she pours to her feet. Steam buries the room in soft heat and fogs the mirror. Time is unknown and irrelevant to her, a moving realm outside the walls. Corvus thinks, I am the only one now. She makes the water hotter and stands for a long time without moving against the black-and-white checkered tiles, still holding the thin neck of the glass between her two fingers. Amber jiggles the doorknob and lets herself in. Corvus, knowing Amber is just on the other side of the curtain, still does not budge from her little private dream. She turns the water even hotter.

Tilting her head, Amber approaches and sits on the closed toilet seat, adoring the unaffected silhouette. She asks the shadow, Can I sit here? May I sit here?

The small square of a room is hot, even the hand lotion bottle is hot. Amber dabs some in her palms and rubs a layer up and down her arms and neck. Corvus pokes her head out of the small gap in the shower curtain, her face partly masked with dangling wet hair, and shows a thumbs-up.

Sure, she says. You can do whatever you want.

Corvus hands Amber the dripping wet glass.

Amber says, Champagne for my real friends. She crosses her legs and listens to the running water, listlessly gazing at the hanging towel on the wall. For a long time, they're silent, which Corvus admires. It's a tiny science: how to be quiet, and when to break it. Her fingers prune under the water.

Corvus asks, Where are we now?

I have an idea.

What?

Amber smiles and says, I have an idea. Wait.

Wait, what?

Amber stands up and talks to the shadow before going ahead and opening the curtain, startling Corvus.

Do you, Amber asks, have anywhere you need to go to? Do you want me to drive you home?

I don't have anywhere, says Corvus. The water is louder than her voice.

Do you want to keep working, then? Keep working with me?

Corvus turns off the water and brushes past Amber reaching for her towel. She wraps it around herself and asks, What are you thinking?

I know Tim's distributor, a woman with black hair. Her

name is Molly, but she goes by Camila, I don't know why. She owns a mansion even deeper in the woods. I really like her.

Corvus asks, What do you like about her?

Amber says, I've always felt like I've known her for a long time. I knew she loved me right away. She told me her house was my house.

Mansion.

Amber makes a crooked, confused face.

Corvus takes off her towel and starts to dry her hair and says, Her mansion is your mansion.

Amber makes eye contact with Corvus in the mirror. She smiles and says, Yes, and it's waiting for us.

Returning the smile, Corvus blissfully cowers in a small, sudden fit of laughter, before catching her breath. She says, Real pain for my sham friends. I don't care anymore. How far?

Not far.

Fuck it, let's go disappear again.

Amber almost screams and says, You're so fun.

Suddenly, a loud knock on the door startles Corvus. Loud pangs, rattling the hinges. The big puppy runs to the door but doesn't bark. He seems ready to pounce, easing his weight on his hind legs. Amber skips over and Corvus moves away from the door.

Sliding the door chain unhooked, Amber says, You're a loud knocker.

The delivery boy looks as though in his teens, sort of bowing to Amber. I'm really sorry, says a deep voice. He holds up two paper bags wrapped inside plastic bags, with HONG's, a dragon, and Chinese characters written on the sides. The bags are dripping wet. The dog stays in place, wagging his tail, never taking his eyes off the delivery boy.

Amber asks, How old are you? How come you're not in school?

Marco: his name tag. Marco nods and says, There are no other cars in the parking lot. I think you guys are the only ones out here.

Creepy, Amber says. Here. She hands him a fifty but doesn't let go until he makes eye contact with her again. They lock eyes and she says, You didn't answer my question?

Marco nods and says, It's, it's Saturday morning.

She lets go and says, Keep the change, Marco, and closes the door, nudging the dog away with her bare foot. Meek and lowly, his footsteps down the stairs and back to the car are as though never heard. His radio starts with the ignition: "Dancing on My Own."

Corvus walks over to the bed, watching Amber set up paper plates on the linen. She pours steaming hot rice onto each plate, then prawns, sweet-and-sour chicken, beef chow fun, and tiny egg rolls. The dog, so good, still does not budge but watches with his entire body. Amber takes a joint out of her purse and, tiptoeing on the queen bed, disables the smoke alarm. She takes a single deep hit, her eyes flickering, and then balances the burning roach on the edge of the alarm clock. Silently, Corvus watches Amber devour her portion of the food, mixing everything into a greasy, lumpy mound. Amber tosses the puppy an egg roll, chews, and coughs smoke, searching for a napkin with her fingers.

Corvus touches her chest unconsciously and smiles in delight. Poor Marco, she thinks. The alarm clock reads 9:27 a.m. Amber swallows and says, I can tell we're going to have an adventure today. I can really feel it. A faraway look comes to her face, her mouth half-full of beef chow fun.

The air smells of weed and coconut sunscreen. Corvus stands slouched, back in time in her head, with no touch of fear on her face. Time travel is as simple as not blinking. Standing with Perry only a few years ago, in her mind, they're checking into a motel just like this one: with a joint in his pocket, he bumps his hips into her hips just to make her laugh. It takes a little longer than usual for Corvus to get her head back to the present, wishing first to dematerialize, before appearing whole in the room again, ready for whatever. Mouth and eyes, back in the room.

Realizing the dog has no name, they decide to name him Marco, and they smile as they watch him in the rearview mirror. The road is bumpy, full of leaves and pebbles. The highway becomes two lanes heading deeper into the woods, and Corvus takes advantage of being in the passenger seat, looking almost all the way up the whole ride, getting lost in the overwhelming canopy of trees. She leans back and pets Marco behind his ear and feels nothing.

Yeah, I only remember Tim calling him Boy or Dog, or he would snap his fingers, Amber says. But nothing else. I don't remember any names for any of his other dogs either, she says. Amber drives too fast, wearing her big sunglasses at the bridge of her nose, and she seems to go even faster around the bends and corners along the cliffs.

I don't either, Corvus says. Let's not talk about Tim anymore.

Corvus looks around and begins to see the water beyond the trees. There is a minor tremor in her left hand. She realizes she hasn't had water yet today, only champagne and coffee and a toke of weed in the morning. Beads of rain blink on the car window as they approach the lake. The light in the fog floats mere inches above the water in small clouds. Corvus turns around: there are no other cars. With the engine off, it is so quiet she can hear her heartbeat; the cold air makes her skin feel dry and alive.

Although Corvus hears a bark in her head, the dog remains quiet in the backseat. He pants and smiles the way dogs do. He doesn't hate me, she thinks. He stares at me. The lake shimmers in dark blue-black patches and secret depths. Amber takes a single breath, as though about to go on camera, and dials an unsaved number on her phone.

Amber listens to the ringing and says, I need a new phone.

Corvus stares at the water and says, Pretty.

There are wooden signs on the dark sand along the shore that read: PRIVATE PROPERTY PLEASE DO NOT SWIM PLEASE DO NOT ENTER THE WATER DELIVERIES PLEASE CALL INVOICE NUMBER. Smaller signs are nailed along the post in different languages and Corvus reads the same message in Spanish. She notes the politeness and the abrupt way the three commands are bunched together.

She turns down the radio: the DJ plays Robyn's "Indestructible." The pop song calms their excited pulses.

Someone picks up. Amber listens, then smiles and says, Camila! Corvus can hear muffled instructions and inaudible language and watches Amber nod and hum and say, Okay, okay, I got it. I missed you, too, I missed you so much. I'll see you in a half hour. Amber hangs up and looks at Corvus. The conversation feels like a homecoming.

This is going to take a bit, she says. Wait here and I'll be right back. Ambers turns up the volume on the radio and mouths along to the lyrics, bopping her head. She reaches for something beneath her seat and comes up with pliers. Amber winks as she exits the car. She walks slightly downhill to a shiny black generator a few yards away, and Corvus sits on her knees to see.

As Amber works, it rains harder. After a long minute, orbs of light begin to illuminate, strung along parallel rows of buoys on the lake, creating a path leading to a now clearly lit view of a house on a close-by island. The house looks massive, even from this distance: a mansion. Amber rises from the ground, a little muddy from work, and Corvus wonders if Amber is a genius. The dog barks once as Corvus clicks her tongue. She decides she loves Amber in this very special way, listening to the sound of her door opening.

There's a canoe, Amber says, wiping her forehead. She nods and looks toward the island. We have to stay in the path.

Corvus asks, Why?

She says, I don't want to scare you.

What?

Amber opens the passenger door to let Marco out of the car. He leaps out and she says, Let's get going and I'll tell you on the way.

Corvus mouths the lyrics, turning the keys free and killing the radio.

Amber walks over to the edge of the lake and dips her hands into the water, washing her hands and then face, suddenly looking incredibly worn down. As she rises, blood rushes to her head. She sees white and then the lake. She looks as though there are a few things wrong, her mind occupied with strange out-of-place scents. Things are here that weren't here before and the place feels larger than she remembers, danker and warmer too. Inside, her chest bobbles.

Marco, without warning, jumps into the black lake. He surfaces farther away than Corvus imagines he could swim in a single breath. She has never seen a dog keep his head underwater for so long before. Marco keeps swimming toward the island and becomes difficult to see in what little waves the lake makes.

He was born in that mansion, says Amber, her voice stern behind Corvus. He and all his brothers and sisters, the whole litter, she says, were all born in that deep basement over there.

Corvus stops at the edge of the sand, each tiny wave rising insignificant magnitudes higher on the shore, and loses sight of Marco. She can see lights glowing from the mansion, and some look like real fire. The building shimmers. She can hardly believe the sight: the foggy view of the brightly lit mansion swarmed by fresh night and black water seems like something from one of her favorite pop songs. As though pulled by the lights, Corvus walks to the beached canoe and, arms crossed, she kicks the hull.

The path is sweet and inviting, she says. The dangers reveal themselves almost immediately.

Amber walks over and touches Corvus's lower back. She asks, Is that from something? Are you quoting a book?

I'm just talking to myself.

Yes. Amber nods emphatically.

It's safe as long as we stay inside the buoys, Amber says.

What's outside the buoys?

Amber hugs Corvus tightly, sinking into the wet sand with her bare toes. She whispers, Nothing to worry about, Corvus.

Corvus notes her own name, softly spoken in Amber's voice, and grows quiet. The wind blows rogue sand particles and droplets of lukewarm water. Amber picks up two spear-length paddles and shrugs her shoulders. Let's canoe, honey, she says.

With no life jackets in sight, they climb inside the canoe, with Amber at the rear, looking loose and comfortable and very much in her element. With almost no effort, they push off, and start paddling. Slowly, they tread and pull a thousand ripples along with them toward the island.

At first, the sound of the water is so soothing, Corvus closes her eyes for a few moments. The tension in her neck melts away with the sounds of the lake. Then she opens her eyes. There is a sense something is happening underwater, like something is underneath the canoe. Corvus can hear deep bellows—animal sounds so guttural and alarming that she prepares her body by gripping the side of the hull. She slows her breath, ready for the canoe to flip. But despite the rippling water, the vessel never does. The deep bellows continue around them and Corvus feels as though the lake could reach up and touch her. Her whole body tightens.

Corvus asks, What is that, Amber? What's that sound?

I feel really tired, Amber says.

We can just drift if you want, Corvus says. Or I can paddle by myself. She breathes herself calm and still, realizing she has been shaking.

Amber stops paddling and lights her last joint, hands cupping the flame from the wind. They pass the roach back and forth silently, at rest on the waves, bright star clusters reflecting in the black water. With Corvus looking up and Amber staring down, the glow of the universe surrounds them in the fog, buried in the alien noise of what lies underwater. Outside the lines of buoys, Corvus can see eyes.

On the other side of the lake, Marco is waiting patiently on a small grassy hill, his tail wagging and still dripping water from the swim. A good boy, he doesn't bark and waits with his mouth open. The bright orbs continue on land, moving from buoys on water to thick standing lamps on shore leading to the entrance, an ornate wrought-iron gate covered in vines of bright yellow and orange flowers. Behind the gate, the mansion on the hill emerges like a mountain, its gigantic white pillars also covered in flowering vines.

Corvus puts her hands on her waist and realizes she is out of breath. The sand sticks to her feet and sore ankles. Amber pulls the canoe away from the water and the growing current and clicks her tongue. Marco barks once and obediently runs down the hill, ears and wrinkles of fur and skin flapping wildly. Like he was never absent from her side, Marco looks up at Amber with his strangely skinny tongue hanging from one side of his mouth, appearing more relaxed and youthful than she's seen him in a long time.

Good swim? she asks. He doesn't make a noise but seems eager to say something. He rolls on his back and starts being funny, eyes wide open. There is a bloodstain on his coat, but from what Amber can tell, it isn't his own blood. She touches the stain and Marco makes no outcry, there's no wound. He looks happy and at peace.

Not far from where they are standing, there is another bloodstain on the concrete near the gate. It looks as though something was repeatedly bashed over and over again into the ground. Bits of red, smashed matter. Everything else within view, even the intricate design of the shiny chrome gate, appears to be polished clean except for this one savage spot. Corvus walks closer, beads of sweat blinking on her collarbone and forehead, and looks through the gaps of the fence. Tall trees and lush gardens guard the other side: dahlias, peonies, and anemones. The ornate perimeter appears to stretch forever around the mansion.

A strong wind picks up and shakes the branches. They can hear the sound of a squeaky door opening farther up the hill. There is a figure walking out of the mansion down the marble path to the gate, hidden in the dark. The footsteps are heavy boots. There are waves rippling in the lake behind them and all kinds of splashing sounds. Corvus can hear snorting and deep breathing not far from the shore. She gently holds the back of Amber's neck and pulls her in. She says, I can hear something. I can hear something. Can you hear that?

Still holding Amber's neck, Corvus squeezes tighter and asks, Amber, what's out there? What the fuck?

You can see.

I can see?

Moans, bellows, and huffing and puffing sounds create a dome around them, as though Corvus and Amber are surrounded. Corvus looks to her left then right and then left again. Past the lamps, on the other side of the line of buoys and thin nets underwater, large, shiny wet mammals are surfacing from the black water and walking on shore toward the woods in darkness. Unable to make out what they are, Corvus holds her breath and grips her chest with her tired hand. Approaching the light, Amber blocks Corvus's line of sight. The wild animals crowd and muscle and grunt past the lamps.

Hippos, says Amber.

What the fuck, Corvus says.

Hippos, says Amber.

Hippos?

Hippopotamuses, says Amber. Hippopotame.

They spend their lives in water, says a new voice.

A woman in a red robe and boots approaches the gate from the mansion. In one hand, she holds an unopened bottle of champagne, and in the other, an empty glass. The robed woman says, That's actually a common mistake, a misconception. They spend *a lot* of their time in water. They like walking around on land, too, only at night, though.

She enters a code into a number pad on her side of the fence and the gate unlocks with a mechanical, echoing screech. Suddenly, the island lights up around them: the streetlamps glow brighter, searchlights appear in the trees, tiny embedded garden lights open in the ground, and kerosene torches burst alive like a consciousness across the property.

Amber says, Camila. Marco barks.

Turning around, Corvus can see the hippos slowly walking to the shadow of the woods beyond the mansion, a few even running there, save for one very large male walking comfortably to the entrance, snorting visible puffs into the cold air. Corvus looks at him approaching in the grass, then back to the red spot on the concrete, and walks over to look at the debris. Camila opens the gate and slips through.

She says, That's where I smash heads.

Amber says, Camila. This is Corvus. Marco barks.

The large male walks over to Camila, not five yards away from Corvus, who cannot stop staring. The rest of the pod are heading to the woods and Camila makes a gesture with her hand to the largest hippo, a motion of patting the air as though saying *simmer down*, and the animal stays. Camila makes eye contact with Corvus and says, Hi, Corvus. Corvus, this is Valerie, my alpha male. They're not usually this friendly.

The animal remains docile, his wet ears flicking away hungry gnats. He seems so big, it's as though he's still moving, his fat and skin shiny and mesmerizing.

Camila says, Corvus, I know your work. I like you. Welcome to my home.

Camila says, Are you okay, Corvus? You look like you're going to faint.

Corvus says, I'm not going to faint.

I know, says Camila. I said you just look like it.

Corvus says, Hi, Valerie. She is nearly hyperventilating; her collarbone rises up and down with her lungs. Valerie blinks his black eyes and yawns, opening his jaw four feet wide. Corvus says, Hi, Valerie, and faints on the concrete, scraping a spot on her elbow bloody as she hits the ground. Marco barks.

CHAPTER 8

CORVUS WAKES UP SORE IN A SILK ROBE IN A LARGE BED
with fresh sheets and a fluffy comforter. She doesn't remember
what she dreams of anymore. It has been that way for years
now, but it no longer bothers her. There is something peaceful
in not knowing. Waking up without dreaming is like taking off
a black mask. No longer feeling grimy or stressed out, Corvus
keeps her body still and takes a moment to realize where she
is. The ceilings are high and the walls are painted a faded gold.
Her elbow is bandaged in white gauze. She is not dead, she is
alive. Corvus takes solace in the fact that there is nowhere she
needs to be, nowhere she needs to go. She lies in bed and listens
for any signs of life within or beyond the walls.

    She misses Perry. Like a panic, she misses Perry with her
whole being, and it's suddenly as though her body is a kind
of costume, and there's something missing between who she

is and whatever is walking around empty in the world. She wishes for his smell, for his strong legs to wrap around hers. It's as though she's been freezing for much too long a time, always cold in her hands and feet, unable to get warm and somehow, now she's colder. Grief is this strange chill, a dead space where there was once fire and comfort, and she fears there is no relief coming.

Someone knocks on the door. Corvus feels a little dizzy and her vision doubles before there is a second knock, this time with the door opening. She loosens her grip on the comforter, taking long blinks. The wound itches under the gauze.

Camila enters the room and says, I'm sorry I don't have someone here for you. She sits down in a wicker chair and scoots closer to the headboard. It's the off-season, so all my help is gone. She waits and asks, How is the elbow? How dreadful.

Corvus doesn't say anything.

Camila asks, Should I leave and let you rest a little while longer?

Where's Amber? Corvus asks. She gets up on her elbows, trying not to grimace from the sting, and sits up.

She's coming, my dear.

Corvus asks, Where the fuck is Amber?

Camila says, She's coming. The pain on her face is visible. It's as though Corvus has committed an intimate and great offense, asking for someone else. Camila straightens her back and smiles at Corvus. She rises from the wicker chair and yells down the hallway, Amber! Amber!

Amber's voice calls back from downstairs. She screams, Yes?

Camila doesn't say anything else, and after a few moments, footsteps rush up the stairs from down the hallway. Amber appears on the threshold, already smiling with her bright eyes. Nothing is strange or out of sorts on Amber's face. She looks relaxed and at ease, as though she's at home here, and the comfort almost brings Corvus to tears.

Amber says, You look good, Corvus. She runs to the bed on excited feet, wearing the same kind of silk robe as Corvus, and leans to her ear still smiling. Amber whispers, We did it, we're safe and chill here.

Camila has stepped out into the hallway, where she stands patiently with her arms crossed, the faded gold paint on the walls matching her gold-painted fingernails. Amber looks at Corvus and nods. She says, It's good here. Better pay, better place.

Amber leans closer and whispers, And we're the only ones here. Just us three. Camila says we can sleep on it and we can sign new contracts for new films whenever we feel like it. She whispers even more softly, And the shoots will be just us two. It's the off-season. Camila is making a special exception.

Corvus says, Just us.

Amber says, You and me. Sometimes Camila, but it's very rare.

Corvus says, Wait a minute.

Amber kisses her forehead and says, I'm so sorry. I left something in the oven downstairs, I'll be right back!

Amber runs out of the room and yells, You can sleep on it! Her footsteps pound from wood to marble to inaudible and nothing. Camila, too, is gone, absent from the doorway. The room almost floats without their faces. Corvus wipes her mouth with her hands and jumps from the bed, surprised by her sudden strength and the immediate rush of blood to her head. The hardwood floor is cold, and she wraps the robe closer to her body as she heads to the hallway. She unwraps her bandage and lets the rags fall to the ground. The wound does not look raw and is already healing in a scab. It doesn't disgust her.

Around the corner, as if expecting her, Camila approaches with a tray of cheese and crackers, champagne and orange juice. Near her knees, Marco follows, with five other almost identical dogs following behind.

Camila says, You've been out nearly two days.

Corvus asks, Why are you doing this for us?

Are you ordinary? Are you run-of-the-mill? No, says Camila quickly. I tried to tell you when you arrived. I know your work and I want to get to know you and offer you a proposal. I think you're special, dear.

Corvus says, You don't know me.

Camila comes closer and whispers, Can I explain myself? The magnetism tickles, her voice gets a little deeper.

Corvus says, Okay.

They go back into the room and clink glasses filled with orange bubbly. All the dogs sit in the same position, watching flying songbirds outside the window. Camila says, Cheers, dear. Silently, at first, they drink.

Corvus watches Marco, wanting to will him to come and

sit next to her but he doesn't move. She is not even completely certain she knows which dog is Marco, so she clicks her tongue, causing Camila to laugh, choking on her champagne.

Not one dog reacts, six panting tongues, six faint shadows on the floor.

Do you know that feeling? Someone you know surprises you. That feeling when someone you know—and it's someone you're not particularly close to, this isn't your best friend, just an acquaintance—they shock you. They take you by complete surprise. They say something so true and so poignant about you, it's a sledgehammer. It wakes you up. And it's just a small thing, dear, whatever they say, it's just some small detail about you. How you laugh, a mannerism, a tell, they translate your body language back to you. And it doesn't matter what they say really, it's more the fact they noticed, this more or less stranger has been watching you and admiring you. They were watching you this whole time and you were unaware. This suddenly beautiful stranger.

Camila takes another sip of her mimosa, finishing the glass. Amber picks up a knife, walks past Corvus to the windowsill, and cuts a piece of apple pie, which is still steaming in the breeze. She takes a bite and gives the plate to Camila, who mouths, Thank you, dear.

Camila says, That's who Amber was for me, someone who just appears in your life, someone who was always there. We were on set one evening, I believe it was five years ago or something, and she was darling. I realized we'd never spoken before and all that changed soon after that night. Camila claps her hands free of crumbs. Walking around the room, she collects their plates and clears her throat. Leaning in, she says, I'm sorry if I scared you with the hippopotamus. Really, I am.

Corvus forks her pie, taking cheese from Amber's plate. Corvus nods and says, That's okay, it was just incredibly unexpected. I've never seen a hippo before. The metal fork scratches the plate.

They're great protection, says Camila. Her eyes are green, dilated, and sparkling. Camila rubs the back of Corvus's shoulder and walks over to a large armoire and opens the top drawer. Corvus can smell marijuana as the breeze reaches her.

They're terribly grumpy, territorial creatures, says Camila, revealing a clear glass pipe. Before I bought them, I watched one snap a crocodile in half with just one snap of his jaw. Right in front of me, she says. It was one of the most visceral things I had ever seen. Blood in the water rippling out everywhere. Four-thousand-pound, aggressive vegetarians.

Amber says, I don't think they're vegetarians. I've heard they eat meat sometimes.

So perfect to guard my island, Camila says, lighting the bowl with a match, and I enjoy watching them. She hands the pipe to Amber and lifts her head and blows smoke to the high ceiling. The smoke clouds and disappears. You just can't treat them like they won't erupt, says Camila. Her eyes grow red and more dilated. Because they will erupt, she says, just like how any one of us can erupt, and explode.

Amber holds up the cheese and says, I've never had this before.

Camila looks back and says, It's really good.

Corvus forks more pie and sticks a piece of cheddar on top. Corvus says, Amber, you did that, so I did that.

Amber chews and says, It's really good, this cheese-and-pie combo.

Corvus asks, Where did you get them?

The cheese?

Corvus says, The hippos. Camila hands the pipe to her and Corvus takes a match. Camila and Amber suddenly look at each other and pause. They start laughing loudly together, almost in perfect unison. Corvus lights the pipe and closes her eyes.

Camila says, You won't believe me.

Corvus asks, What? Try me.

Camila looks at Amber then back to Corvus and says, Pablo Escobar.

What are you talking about?

Amber says, No, listen. For real.

Pablo Escobar, says Camila, mainly because he wanted them there, housed countless pods of aggressive hippos on his main living estate in Colombia. When his empire fell, the hippos remained, and the Colombian government had no idea what to do with this non-native species. They started the desperate messaging of: *Free if you take them from us.* Zoos, scientists, billionaires, and other interested parties all heeded the call.

Corvus says, And porn stars.

Camila says, And adult entertainment moguls, yes. I can have hippos too, my dear. I can have hippos if I damn well want them.

Corvus reaches for the pipe and smiles and says, The lives we live.

Camila says, I know no other way.

Amber asks, What are we doing tonight? The windows glare with sunlight, the lake shimmers on the horizon. Corvus can't see anything but water. Above them, as in nearly all the rooms, the mirrored ceilings reflect the glowing chandeliers. Tiny burning candlesticks. They smoke and can't feel a thing.

Camila says, Party, dear. We are going to party.

After night falls, Corvus explores the island beyond the mansion. Stepping into the line of glowing lamps, she can see the island is special. Gigantic art structures come into view, and, along her walk, she finds garden mazes scattered throughout the property. Corvus imagines spending the rest of her life in this place, growing old, walking this strange island. The moonlight on the lake shimmers and draws her closer. She passes by a row of black marble dog statues, each the size of a Toyota Corolla. They all look like Marco. Corvus approaches one on the wet grass and touches the cold statue. I love you, Marco, she says.

High on a marble land bridge, Corvus watches the hippos from a safe distance, and looks up at the moving blackness accumulating in the sky. It looks like rain and more. She plays a game she used to play when she was younger, something she used to do to distract herself from her mother. Corvus imagines the wind breaking her apart during a storm: each breeze carries off just a microscopic bit of her; each breeze takes her a little farther away into the atmosphere until all that's left of her is her mind glowing alone in a vacuum, no longer really thinking, no longer in pain. There is freedom in believing you are through, in giving up, in believing there is nothing left to do with yourself. Corvus looks to the beach. If possible, she thinks, she could stay here forever.

The black clouds overhead keep moving and forming. Strangely, the hippos float single file on the lake. Corvus leans on the railing and wonders which one is Valerie. They don't seem to be aware of her looking at them from above. A wave of nausea moves through her with the wind as she watches the pod. She trembles in her favorite sweater.

Footsteps approach. Certain moments fill her heart with sharp adrenaline, such as suddenly having to speak with strangers. Camila walks closer with a sway to her hips, her finger gliding along on the cold railing. Corvus turns to look, and when she turns her head back around, she can no longer make out the hippopotamus. She leans farther over the railing, but Corvus can only see murky water, a thousand tiny waves. No hippos.

Camila walks the length of the bridge toward Corvus, neither making eye contact with the other.

They're under, dear. They've submerged, haven't they? They do that from time to time, Camila says. Time after time. Her eyes look all black in this light, her hair whips back and forth in the wind.

Corvus loses herself in sudden peals of laughter, and covers her mouth smiling. Muffled, she says, What the fuck am I doing here? She looks for the hippos in the water and shakes her head with no answer. The laughter hurts in a good way, right in the soft pit of her stomach.

I used to try really hard to get people to like me, Camila says. My whole life. I remember I was always this polite, accommodating little thing. Do you know what I'm talking about, my dear? The wind blows a little more calmly now.

Corvus feels a current between them, some kind of spark or connection, curious and generous. She chews nothing but teeth and asks, What do you mean?

Camila takes out a pocket knife, snaps the blade open, and slices the air around her. She says, I mean getting taken advantage of. I mean not getting your due, dear. Camila slices repeating figure eights in the ghostly fog and carries on the conversation as normal, playing with the knife. She says, I started to take care of myself. I was so tired of catering to the needs of other people.

Corvus nods absently, and she eyes Camila's blade. Briefly, a little suspicion needles her neck.

I see that in you, Camila says. You have the walk of a defeated person. Camila spins the knife in the air but anticipates too early, and she catches the wrong end, cutting her hand. Camila says, I saw you tonight and I thought, Maybe this girl has seen something, maybe she is grieving.

Corvus thinks, I *am* grieving. She listens to the wind and points to Camila's bleeding hand.

Don't worry about it, dear, says Camila, shrugging off the sting. The blood drips in a small pool on the marble. She says, I became my own woman. I became this house, this mansion, this island.

Corvus asks, These hippos?

Watch it, dear, says Camila. Don't be a smart-ass. Camila is still holding the wrong end of her pocket knife. What I mean is, I know what grief is, too. I can see it in you, she says. Camila's face is visibly stricken, not from physical pain, but as though wincing from a memory.

Is that why you changed your name? Corvus asks. Amber said your name used to be Molly.

Ignoring her, Camila says, What I mean is, you can stay here on the island and be at peace. You can do anything you want here. If you can just leave things at peace, in the past. You can stay here.

Corvus says, Thank you, and stops herself from saying anything else.

Camila closes the knife and starts wrapping her palm with the scarf she has around her neck, already soaking up the blood. She says, I still can't feel my face.

Corvus asks, What were you and Amber huffing when I was leaving for my walk?

Novocain, says Camila, no longer looking sad. I have tanks and tanks of it, she says. You can have some when we get back.

Of course, Corvus says, her voice breaking a little. They start walking back to the mansion. The air is frigid and biting, the water shimmers behind them like diamonds. Thank you,

Corvus says, and she holds the front door to the mansion open, her hand shaking on the grip, the fatigue from the walk finally catching up with her.

No one else has been invited to this party, says Camila, and it's wonderful, just the girls and no unknown variables. There is bubbly poured, glasses raised, and all the women are sprawled out on couches, watching wood burn in the fireplace. Corvus cannot help feeling like she now has fragile access to a lost portal or tiny hole in time, some place intimate and tucked away, uncharted and left alone by other people. It's the same reason she has always loved bunk beds, treehouses, towers, and secret rooms and compartments: the privacy is perfect. Corvus imagines herself walking the perimeter of the island alone every day for years, walking in sunshine, rain, and snow, the calm lake on one side of her, old-growth trees and garden mazes on the other. In her mind's eye, she can live here. She can be at peace here in her own way.

Fuck first, says Camila's voice. We have to fuck first. Don't you know about *fuck first*, dear?

Corvus turns around and sees Amber in the middle of a deep stretch, breathing deeply, her foot nearly arched to the back of her head: a yoga pose. Camila has her hands on Amber's exposed, toned abdomen, looking as though she wants to melt into Amber. She looks really high.

Amber says, Sometimes after I've done this pose, I've cried uncontrollably for hours. With her eyes unblinking, Amber brings her foot all the way to her ear, and exhales through a small *o* in her mouth. Her pupils water and she looks sad. She says, I don't know what it is. Maybe my childhood.

Gently letting her hands go, Camila says, That's quite dark, my dear.

Corvus asks, What were you talking about, Camila? *Fuck first?*

Oh, yes. Itinerary, says Camila. She leads Marco to a door in the kitchen that leads to the basement, where the studio, filming equipment, props, and sets are kept, where Marco likes to sleep, and Camila shuts him inside. The door is padlocked, but not completely soundproof: Corvus can hear Marco obediently climbing down the stairs. Camila taps the door and says, We'll be down there soon enough.

She says, Contracts. Drugs. Champagne. Feast. The first video. Camila counts with her fingers, hovering an open hand at the end of the list of things to do. Amber and Corvus watch her curiously. While talking, Camila pours dry food into six silver dog bowls.

Camila says, I have every drug in the world, just ask. Don't be shy, dear. Also, I am a masterful chef, and tonight, I am cooking all of us a feast. I'm thinking four or five courses just for the fuck of it. We can drink, get stoned, and then go out to my Jacuzzi on the rooftop.

Corvus and Amber look at each other silently and smile.

Camila snaps her fingers and appears serious. She says, But I have a rule: we have to fuck first.

Amber starts laughing but keeps it muffled with her hand.

Instead of eating all that food, drinking, and smoking first, I like having sex first, to get it out of the way, Camila says. And in that order, the sex won't be as gross and bloated and blurry afterward. I swear by it, dear.

Corvus says, No, that's really smart.

So I figured, says Camila, we can go downstairs and have some fun, shoot our first video together. I can show you my directing style and how we operate here, and we can go from there.

Corvus looks at Amber, but realizes Camila is addressing her directly. Hesitantly, Corvus says, Okay. Contracts?

Camila walks over, hands Corvus a dog bowl, and rubs her bare shoulder. She says, We can do the paperwork after the fun.

Amber leaps in the air, her hair blooms and falls. Her bare feet make a faint squeak on the kitchen floor.

Camila says, Here, dear. Let's each get two bowls and bring the food to the dogs. We can start filming right after.

She unlocks the padlock and goes down first, followed by Amber and then Corvus. Immediately, walking down the steps, Corvus can see the basement is much larger than she imagined, and still under construction. She sees spare pieces of plywood abandoned on the floor in random piles, tarps, and a wheelbarrow of cement. Each room leads to another; Camila turns on more lights, revealing more doors. She says, Let's leave the bowls here. I want to show you the studio.

There is a blue door and a black door. The black door opens to a larger room, what appears to be a small black box theater. Nothing is inside: the walls are painted black, the acoustics in

the room are sharp and crisp. Camila says, We're going to the
studio next to this one. It's a black box too, but the cameras are
there, and the beds and toys are all set up.

Camila opens the blue door, letting Amber and Corvus
go in first. There are booths and white curtains set up, with a
bed and camera inside each empty porn set. The space looks
more surgical than erotic. Corvus turns her head and sees all
six dogs asleep in the corner of the theater. She smiles and says,
There they are.

With a bright smile on her face, Amber walks over to the
sleeping dogs, approaching one of the sets. Behind her, the
white curtains move open and a figure appears. The figure steps
out from the curtains and there is a smack in the air. Amber's
head knocks forward as she collapses to the floor. Through the
open curtain, Tim stands staring at Corvus, holding a broomstick, Amber unconscious at his feet. The broom handle is made
of solid gold.

Corvus says, Holy shit.

Camila screams, Tim! What the fuck did you do to my
dogs? Camila stands blocking the only exit. Her pocket knife
shows in the palm of her hand.

Corvus says, Holy shit.

Tim says, Relax. They're only asleep. They wouldn't stay
quiet so I used tranquilizers. Tim pulls one out of his pocket
and takes the red cap off the needle point. He looks Corvus in
the eye and says, I know what's going to happen to you. But
you don't.

PART TWO

LIFE WITH PERRY

CHAPTER 1

IT'S A MOMENT THAT ACTUALLY HAPPENS TO HER: SHE CAN trace back to how she used to be. She remembers being afraid of almost everything: walking home by herself at night, being poor and stuck and awkward, making small talk. But the fear doesn't happen now and she's on her own separate plane. She doesn't care. It's an amazing thing: meeting someone, making a connection, letting someone talk to you. Corvus ends the conversation with the boy she doesn't know by getting up, carefully browsing and choosing a new record, and dancing by herself in the middle of the room. The song beeps in her chest, and Corvus gets lost in her own dancing, the thrill of no special occasion. The dance floor lights up, and other bodies swarm around. The hardwood floor vibrates beneath her feet to the bass, signals and tingles rise to her brain. The boy watches from the couch a little openmouthed, as Perry enters the room with two drinks, Michelle right behind him.

They all live together: three roommates, two lovers, one household. Michelle starts dancing like she was already here, surveying the ether. Corvus keeps dancing and touches Michelle's ear and says, Sometimes, life gives you a moment. Michelle rolls her eyes and barely nods.

That boy over there was trying to flirt with me.

Michelle asks, Which boy?

Perry sits on the couch next to the boy and lights a cigarette. The music is at a rise, and the bodies ahead of them in the smoky dark sway, bump, and grind against one another. Corvus backs up and pushes Michelle against the vibrating wall. They mouth the chorus together.

The boy says, Hey. What the fuck. He coughs from the cigarette smoke.

Perry leans back on the couch and tries to pull his phone out of his pocket, but his pants are too tight. The phone makes a square bulge in the denim and Perry gestures at the shape. He says, Pants are too tight.

The boy says, Dude. We're inside. He keeps coughing.

Perry says, I live here. This is my house. I pay a mortgage.

The boy says, Okay.

Okay, says Perry. Perry drinks from his cup and looks ahead.

Michelle, close to Corvus's ear in the fuzzy dark, says, I think that dude is talking to Perry.

The boy rubs his hands together and says, You should be mindful about your guests. He waves away the smoke.

Perry slowly turns his head around and says, I don't know you. Smoke cycles through his mouth and nostrils.

Radiating with a temper, the boy clenches his fists. He tries to lunge at Perry but is stopped by heavy hands that hold him down on the couch, heavy hands from heavy men standing up above him. The boy looks up behind him and the men look dead serious, one gripping and digging deeper into his shoulder.

Perry says, See, that's the thing about privilege.

The boy grimaces in pain and grips his chest; the men lift him off his seat effortlessly, deadpan and serene faces on both of them. The boy's feet are off the ground, his shadows are kicking.

Perry says, It makes you feel like the world is for you. And the world is not for you.

The boy mouths, What?

The man with the softer grip says, The world is not for you, son.

They carry him out the back door to the street, opening the door with his head. Perry leans back and says, Thanks, to no one in particular. The lights dim. The next song on the record is even louder, and there are more bodies, more stomachs, more legs and thighs. Perry isolates the noises and hears the pop song and the sounds of traffic outside simultaneously. Corvus sways to the couch and leans her head on Perry's shoulder.

She says, Hi.

He says, Hi.

After two more songs, Corvus closes her eyes, and Michelle walks over, sits close, and rests her head on Corvus's shoulder, speaking nonsense before passing out almost right away. The wind blows to no end, down to the very last drunk-ass guest.

•

She wakes up dreamless in the black, opening her eyes to sunlight on her face, her favorite way of waking up. This is the third night in a row Corvus has fallen asleep in the living room. She wakes on the futon that she never pulls out, and this time there aren't small piles of people scattered all around her. Instead, just Michelle is sleeping soundly on her shoulder, which makes Corvus smile, but Perry is nowhere to be seen. She stretches and straightens her back on the couch cushions without waking Michelle and looks around for signs of Perry. But there's nothing, not even a trace from last night's party: the place has already been tended to and tidied. Immaculate and clean. He always does this, she whispers.

Books are straightened and grouped by color, the floors and tables are swept, and fresh tulips appear in recycled wine bottles on every other windowsill. There's a small cookie jar shaped like a happy gnome full of leftover cocaine, pill bottles, and loose nuggets of marijuana that Perry leaves on the coffee table with a handwritten note: I LOVE YOU, I LOVE YOU. TURN THIS NOTE OVER.

Corvus turns the note over to read the same message and smiles. She digs into a rogue bag of potato chips and finds the last good one and licks the salt from her fingers. She knows where he is, so she doesn't call for him. She waits for the sound and finds it: keys bouncing on a lanyard, tapping against a coatrack. Whenever Perry runs on his treadmill, nearly the entire basement shakes, and he always leaves his keys in the same place: hanging on the coatrack where the cheap plywood floor is the weakest. Still licking her fingers, she opens the door to the basement and gets a vague feeling of déjà vu as she crosses the threshold; the dim lights are already on downstairs.

The keys tap gently against the wooden coatrack, little jingles, and a Michael Jordan bobble head bobbles on a coffee table. The TV is turned to mute playing the news: a car is on fire and causing heavy traffic downtown. Perry is running hard on the treadmill, unaware she's there, and Corvus sits on the staircase watching him. She can hear soft hip-hop music from his earphones. Pretzel, her old cat, comes up to her quietly, and then purrs in place the moment she gets to Corvus. She leans against a wall, signals for Pretzel to come to her lap, which always works, Pretzel is a good girl, and watches Perry run, sometimes glancing at the news on the TV, or sometimes staring straight through everything at nothing at all. She waits for him to finish, warm with Pretzel cuddling her.

The machine slows down as Perry takes a deep breath and starts to walk for his cooldown. He takes his earphones off, leaving them to dangle from his shirt, and wipes his brow with his sleeve. Perry never sounds like he's hyperventilating, even after running six miles, and Corvus enjoys watching his triceps and listening to him breathing.

Corvus says, Hey.

Perry's head whips back, still walking on the treadmill.

He says, Hey, honey.

Perry leaps off the still-moving conveyor belt and pushes

the red button. Although he's not out of breath, his shirt is drenched, and he smiles when he sees her in full view in the stairway. After so many years together, he's still excited when he sees her. The sad man has a happy face.

She comes closer and Perry warns her, I'm really sweaty. Corvus hugs him even harder than she had wanted to and smiles against his chest. They walk over to the couch near the mute TV: an ambulance drives off screen. Pretzel jumps up between them, still purring, making eye contact with each of them.

Perry says, I love animals.

Oh, yeah?

Yeah, Perry says. I love animals. I've been watching a lot of videos lately of animals displaying empathy or great sorrow. Like there was this one Rottweiler that wouldn't leave his dead brother's side. It was like ten minutes of this dog nestling against another dog's corpse, and he wouldn't budge. Whimpering.

Corvus says, Poor boy.

Perry says, It makes me sad when I see human traits in animals, the same traits I feel like I don't see in humanity anymore. It makes me feel like we all want something we'll never have. Perry keeps rubbing Pretzel's chin and zones off into the wall.

She looks at him and considers him and says, I love you.

I love you, he says.

Corvus picks up a frame with a photograph from when they first met. There is still some cocaine stuck to the glass. She says, Look at us. Look at all the weight you've lost. Pretzel jumps off her lap and runs away, a furry guided missile. I wish you would quit smoking, though, she says.

Perry gets up and grabs the keys on the lanyard off the wall. He says, Don't you have work soon? I can drive you.

I can walk.

No, honey, I can drive you. No trouble.

Are you sure?

Yeah.

Thanks, honey, says Corvus.

Walking up the stairs, he says, You know, I'm making good money now. You don't have to work anymore.

Corvus looks at him and holds the door open. She says, I like to work. From the kitchen, she can see that Michelle is still asleep on the couch, so she whispers, Hey, who were those two guys from last night? They kicked out the loser.

The tall men?

Yeah.

I think they're fans of the play. They were talking to me about some fan club earlier in the night.

Corvus smiles and blushes and says, That's funny. Really?

Perry laughs and says, Yeah, I couldn't believe it. They told me they had my back forever.

Forever?

Perry says, Yeah, it's pretty weird.

Perry pushes the red button to open the garage door. The ceiling motor grinds, the garage door folds and opens, and Corvus imagines gears turning. As the garage door pulls open, she sees the boy and the two huge men from last night's party standing at the very end of the small paved driveway. They look as though they have been standing there all morning: the two brute men look immovable, and the boy looks like he's freezing to death, shivering as he stands there.

Perry looks stunned, his face is white. He says, What?

Corvus tugs at her shirt as though to hide her chest, and walks quickly over to the standing red tool chest, pulling out a large hammer. She spins the hammer in her hand once. The two men walk the boy up the paved driveway.

I'm sorry to disturb you, Perry, says one of the tall men. He looks at Corvus and says, Corvus. But this boy has something to say. The other tall man nods.

Corvus lowers the hammer to her side and asks, How did you know my name?

The boy from the party tries to talk but no sound comes out of his mouth. He has a black eye, dirt on his shirt, and looks pale. Finally, he says, I'm really, really sorry, Perry. I shouldn't have been so disrespectful last night. I'm really sorry, Perry. The boy walks a little closer. I'm sorry, Corvus.

The boy is too ashamed to look Corvus in the eye, still shivering, although it isn't cold outside.

Corvus spins the hammer in her hand again. Perry says, Okay, okay. Look, we have to go. I have to drive my fiancée to work right now.

Both tall men nod and begin to leave. They tap the boy on the shoulder but he stays standing there, disheveled and sorry. Perry opens the passenger door for Corvus and turns to look back at the boy.

The front door opens, and Michelle appears in her bra and underwear, looking as though she just doesn't care, smoking a joint, to check the mail. She's wearing black slides and she slides down the driveway. The two tall men walk off in rhythm, and Corvus and Perry blow Michelle a kiss and wave goodbye. They drive off with their windows rolled down, bumping the bass loudly on the trunk stereo.

Michelle, bills and advertisements in her hand, walks over to the boy still standing in the driveway. In the sunlight, she considers him and sees he has a tattoo on his neck that reads *tattoo*.

Exhaling smoke, she asks, Is your mother's name Tattoo?

He shakes his head, No.

Then that's fucking stupid. Get off the premises before I call the pigs.

Corvus watches her co-worker eat a ripe banana and forgets what she was doing in the first place. Mary with her stoned eyes and unbuttoned uniform says, I was legally dead for a full minute once. She talks with her mouth full of chewed Skittles and banana. The lobby is empty, air-conditioned, and sun-drenched, the light pouring in from the glass walls. The rusted kettle pops bright yellow kernels and the smell of butter in the air haunts them for the entire shift. No one wants to watch a movie today— this has been the case lately. No shows for five screens.

Corvus says, I know, you've told me before. Lake Erie, right?

No, Mary says, smiling. Lake Crescent. Lake Erie was another story. Mary slips a twenty-dollar bill from the cash register into her pocket, eyes the surveillance camera, then moves to the kettle, scooping and mixing the popcorn together. White and yellow, butter and plain.

Mary says, Only six more hours.

Louis walks over holding a broom and dustpan.

He asks, Do you feel that?

Corvus asks, Feel what?

Louis has been showing signs of affection for Corvus for weeks now. Plus, he's a talker. He likes being a talker. He winks at her, gets a little too close, and Corvus looks openly disgusted. His uniform smells like cigarette smoke and old butter, his white shirt no longer white.

No, I don't feel anything, Corvus says. Perhaps nausea. Yeah, nausea.

I hope you feel better, Louis says.

Corvus walks backward toward the stairs to escape to the projection room. Walking up the flight of stairs, she lifts her eyes to the skylight and imagines flying all the way through to the sky and clouds like a superhero. She can overhear Mary saying, What the fuck is wrong with you? You know it's obvious what you're doing, right? You know she's engaged, right?

Inside the employees' lounge, the size of a closet, Corvus pulls her hair back and takes a codeine pill and slips off her dress. Looking at herself in the spotted mirror, she locks the door and takes off her underwear. Corvus whispers, I'm naked inside a movie theater. She unzips her bag, pulling out her shirt and tie. There is something helpless in putting on a uniform, she thinks, in reading your name on a pin next to a corporate logo.

Fully dressed to company code, she walks with a lint roller to the projection booth. No one is there, and all the shows are underway. Some of the other employees get scared being up there by themselves because the booth is old, rickety, and drafty. Corvus feels as though she could fall through the floor at any moment, or that the ceiling could collapse when she least expects it. The dark seems darker. But Corvus likes the dark, the hums and clicks of the spinning projectors, the squares of light. Every shift, she takes five minutes to walk through the projection booth, and the walk is a meditation.

Movies, movies, fucking movies, she says.

The walls are covered with posters from years and years back. She peeks down each window to each theater and, sadly, no one is seated. The shows play anyway, as scheduled. Lights and sounds for the dank ether.

Corvus knocks on the door of the manager's office. Dick, the manager, doesn't say anything, but Corvus can see his moving silhouette through the closed blinds, so she pushes open the locked door since it's been known to open with a hard shoulder.

Dick does a line of cocaine from his desk, looks up at Corvus, and says, Do you need me down there? He sniffs, then stares at the wall clock, wiping his nose with his black-and-yellow Batman tie. Corvus shakes her head and closes the door behind her. Being perplexed is part of Dick's demeanor. He shakes a vial in the air but Corvus declines and keeps shaking her head. She sits on a swivel chair and spins once.

Can you tell Mary, says Dick slowly, tapping the glass screen of the surveillance monitor, to fucking stop stealing? I can see her clear as fucking day.

Corvus says, You tell her.

I tried to tell her I loved her the other day.

Did you ask her to move in? Wasn't that happening? asks Corvus.

Dick pours out the vial and prepares another line. He turns on the FM radio on the desk. The Brothers Johnson. "Strawberry Letter 23." Dick laughs silently without telling Corvus why, then inhales to capacity.

Feeling a wince in her throat, she asks, Have you been feeling okay? You look dead on the inside.

He says, Being dead on the inside is a talent of mine. He says, And Mary told me she'll think about it. She'll think about it.

Corvus asks, She'll think about it?

Dick nods. She'll think. About it.

Corvus says, Oh. She spins once in her chair, legs crossed. Dick turns down the music and his eyes water. The radio is too low to hear what's playing now.

So what are you doing here? Did you need anything? Dick asks.

I need to get off a little early tonight. Perry has a new play and it's opening tonight.

Dick says, Oh, yeah, shit. I heard the ad on the radio this morning. That's fucking crazy.

What is? asks Corvus.

How famous your fiancé is getting, Dick says, rubbing his hair back. What are you even doing here?

Corvus's face goes cold all of a sudden, and she stiffens up straight in her chair. She has the tendency to go a little cold when people ask her this type of question, and she hates explaining herself. She does what she wants. She lives how she will.

So are we good? She waits, raising her eyebrows.

Dick reaches into his pocket and pulls out another glass vial, one with a happy-face sticker on the lid. He says, Yeah, no worries. Just tell Mary she's closing by herself tonight.

No, Corvus says. Louis the Creep is here.

The lights flicker. There is a knock on the door so forceful, the blinds shake. Corvus is briefly alarmed before she realizes who it is. Corvus and Dick look at each other and shake their heads in unison. She whispers, What the fuck? Speak of the devil.

Dick finishes the cocaine on his desk and howls as Louis comes bursting through the locked door. Louis, reacting to Dick, enters howling.

Louis says, I don't know why you even bother locking this.

I was just leaving, Corvus says, rushing quickly out of the room for the stairs. She makes it. Soon it is as though she was never there.

Louis looks back at Dick after watching Corvus go. Dick wipes his eyes and says, Close the door. He motions with his hands.

Dick keeps wiping his eyes and looks up. He sees Louis still standing there in his office and he says, No. Close the door. With you on the other side.

The house is packed to the top rows, waves of heads and hair and flashes of light. As always, Corvus's seat in the front row is stitched in red cursive: *Reserved Only for Corvus.* Michelle, right next to her, is slumped in her seat in a black dress, eating oily popcorn without a care in the world. When she looks up and exhales, her pupils are bigger than Corvus has ever seen them. They share a smile that mutes the entire auditorium, and under her breath, Corvus feels glee in needles.

Where the fuck did you get popcorn? whispers Corvus. They don't sell that here.

It's from the car, says Michelle. I found it. With her mouth full, eyes glazed, and no shame, Michelle leans farther back against the thin cushion and hugs her knees. Do you want some?

Corvus says, That shit is like three days old. Her smile hurts her face. People are putting their jackets on their seats as ushers look blank-faced along the aisles.

Michelle says, Seventy-two hours. She digs for another handful, faded from brandy. She smiles and says, I'm excited for the show.

They laugh as the house lights dim and die. It's pitch black for perhaps a single second.

A curtain opens. Then another opens. The curtains sweep open to show a black box theater, plain black floors, and an old record player at center stage. It starts to play underneath a single spotlight. An opera. A woman's voice in sorrow. Then two doors open, and two beams of light pour in, stage right and stage left. Nearly naked dancers dressed in what looks to be only white sashes jump on stage and flow in on cue. They are perfectly timed: explosive leaps, all sinew and leg muscle shining and contracting as they hang for so long for so high in the air.

The look on their faces seems to belong to a place very far away from the theater, more up in the clouds than contained in a room. As the opera fades to quiet, the sound of feet landing tremendously to the floor shakes Corvus's core a little. She leans back in her seat and calms herself. She shakes her head, takes a breath.

Michelle leans in and says, Oh my god.

Corvus whispers, Watch.

A little girl walks on stage holding a tape recorder and the dancers keep dancing. They form a circle around her as though protecting her at the center and they go faster. One by one, the sashes fall and reveal scar tissue. Each dancer has some kind of wound, some look raw and painful, wet. Their faces are still and transported. A man and a woman walk in at the other end of the stage and immediately scream at each other, but the dancers keep dancing.

Then a moment: a blue light hovers over the girl and everything else pauses. The screaming stops, the dancing stops. The actors freeze in place, mid-motion, still breathing.

The little girl touches her face and then her chest. She touches her face as though something is missing, as though something has been stolen away, her hands are frantic. The little girl kneels down to the floor. She tries to throw up whatever's there, the universe in her stomach, but only dry heaves. The audience listens to her dry heave for an entire minute. She kicks her head back up and from a secret pocket in her dress takes out and lights a cigarette.

The little girl looks out to the black, scans the audience, and says, I have missed you for years. Exhaling a cloud of smoke from her nostrils and then mouth, she says, For years and years.

She says, I've come to save you. She places the tape recorder on the ground and presses a button.

Perry's voice plays overhead, the blue light goes out:

There were months where I did the same things for weeks at a time. Meals were interchangeable, my outfits moved on and off me, and there were days I had no opinion, my mind blank, walking home alone following palm trees overhead. I remember looking around during different parts of the day: leaving the apartment complex, cruising around the grocery store, reading at a bar after work, having a smoke. Everyone was having a different conversation than I was. All the strangers, everyone was moving quickly in and out of the rooms we were in together, anxious to be somewhere in the future. I was watching and imagining I was away from here: I was gone, walking around with Corvus in Paris, going somewhere to be with friends. I don't know why it was always Paris in the rain.

There were months I felt as though I had no head, or I did the same things for long stretches of time, and it became surreal. Days were less and less about anything. People often refused to make eye contact with one another or looked spaced out. I pretended I was indestructible to pass the time, painting house after house or taking whatever odd job I could find, working seven days a week, and sleeping defeated in bed when I was exhausted. I watched wall clocks and digital timers. Sometimes I would change positions in bed to try something else. My foot would be where my head was, and my head where my foot was. I slept every way I could in my sweet bed, creating solitude from malaise.

I would walk in the daylight without wincing, thinking about Corvus. It was my favorite activity, repeating routines, in uniform or in transit, until I would be closer to her. When we were reunited, it felt so good it was as though I had survived some sort of trauma or natural disaster, being away from her. Although there were days I felt nothing, I could go as cold as nature to the awful things around me. I could be quiet in a room and feel alive.

The building could collapse onto me and I would still tell you I needed to get back home to her.

The tape recorder clicks off. The dancers start dancing again, the man and the woman resume screaming at each other, and the little girl collapses to the floor with a small bounce, still smoking her cigarette. Everything appears to be okay. The dancers never run into one another, limbs and torsos in rhythm, leaping even higher. A wool sweater is thrown out on the floor next to the little girl's body and she reaches out to touch it. Thick fog from a smoke machine rolls on stage, cheesy flashes of purple and blue neon blind the audience: a new act begins.

CHAPTER 2

CORVUS TAKES A STINKY HIT FROM THE SPLIFF AND FEELS lighter, standing in front of a cheering crowd. With one hand on the small of her back, Perry waves to the happy faces. He pulls her hair and gently bites the back of her neck. More cheering. Feeling blissfully transported, Corvus looks at no one in particular and quietly sinks in her bones. The club is bumping and grinding, a hundred arms raise a glass to them. Some drink, some pour it everywhere, beams of light cutting through fizzy champagne sprayed in the air. The DJ, a young woman in a hoodie, pushes up her sleeves and looks Corvus dead in the eyes. Hoodie spins and spins and smiles, then touches buttons, and the crowd turns into a mob, bumping and grinding. Turn down for what. The floor is heaven, the bass draws more and more bodies to the center of the dance floor.

Corvus feels as though she's been here before: almost happy. Almost there. Perry kisses her behind the ear and goes off on his own into the mob, holding his drink in the air. The song has synth hooks. The walls are television screens. Every TV screen is a mouth opening, lips puckering in a Technicolor loop played over and over again. To the beat.

Corvus moves her body through the crowd and shakes, shakes. She knows how terrible she can feel, how bad it can get. But it's really good right now. It's really fucking good right now. In almost complete darkness, she holds up her arms and closes her eyes. Then she brings her arms back down to mask her face and it feels like the greatest thing to do. The fuzzy neon flashes back on, and the beat returns. Everything, everyone around her, is dancing.

A hand grabs her hand, hard at first.

Corvus looks back and it's Perry. He leans in grimacing and says, I'm so sorry.

His face looks anxious, but because it's so dark, it's hard to be sure. From his grip, Corvus can tell that something is bothering him. That the room is irritating him.

The crowd opens slightly. Perry leads Corvus up a staircase, each step lighting up as they escape away from the dance floor. The song is full of rage and sorrow and bodies are sweating all lovely up against each other.

They open a door and enter a private room made of glass, suspended above the dance floor. Barely any sound bleeds through, only mute vibrations. Corvus can hear her heartbeat as she finds a long couch and collapses. She looks up at the chandelier and says, How perfect.

Below, the dancing crowd looks like an ocean of heads and

limbs. Perry walks back from the minibar holding a bottle of champagne.

She takes a glass from Perry.

She can see Michelle in a large men's jacket, swaying back and forth and back and forth. She moves as if her eyes are closed.

Briefly, Corvus thinks about how old she is getting.

Perry pours champagne and taps her glass.

He says, I love you, honey.

I love you, says Corvus.

Corvus leads Perry to the edge of the glass room and looks down. Thick smoke and shiny bodies. She gets a little light-headed and leans her head back. She falls ever so slightly into Perry, and he carries her away in his arms, tossing her goofily onto the couch. Once horizontal, Corvus starts laughing hysterically and Perry falls down next to her, laughing too. Manic, uncontrollable laughter.

Perry asks, What the fuck is happening?

Corvus looks up at the glowing black chandelier and stops blinking.

I think we've made it, she says. I think we're happy.

Shit, Perry says.

Yeah, she says, I think we've made it.

Happy, he says. We're happy.

Perry looks away. Perry looks at Corvus.

We're happy. She can feel herself nodding, she can feel her eyes getting brighter after taking a deep breath. Euphoria warms the blood and her ears pop.

CHAPTER 3

TRANSFIXED BY A HOLE IN HIS SHIRT, CORVUS TELLS PERRY a small white lie: that she saved a man from blindly crossing the street and getting hit by a car. She lies because she doesn't know why—she's bored and it's barely a conscious thing. He's standing in the middle of the kitchen, looking across the living room at a mirror, trying to tie his tie. Pretzel purrs by her feet and twists around her ankles in a figure-eight pattern. A firetruck banshees by; the radio is playing the weekend update.

Perry doesn't ask much about the man almost getting hit by a car, stays quiet, and finishes his knot. He touches her back and kisses her goodbye, and Corvus regrets the white lie almost immediately. They both leave for work, unlocking fingers and departing from the door in opposite directions. She looks at the sky and it's a good sky. Her bus is right on time and it's empty. The clouds move slowly.

•

After a few hours of staring at a blank wall in complete silence in his studio, Perry walks down the fire escape to smoke a spliff. He chooses a spot of torn bricks on the building across the way from his studio and he zones off. His eyes get heavy in his favorite way, and he turns up the music in his headphones. All he needs to do today is write a few pages for a new play. That's all he needs to do today, he thinks. Perry paces the sidewalk and feels a great dread.

If he has time today, he could go for a run. He has to keep up his momentum or all is lost. Perry thinks, If I have time, I'll go for a run. He touches his stomach underneath his shirt on the way to the corner store, feeling his baby fat, stoned and worried.

Walking through the brightly lit convenience store, Perry takes a long time in the freezer aisle. He pays in cash and says thanks to the young clerk, a woman with tattooed sleeves of cityscapes. When she asks him what he's listening to, tapping her ear, Perry writes the name of the musician down on the back of his receipt and leaves the store. It's not until he opens the door to his studio that he realizes he has not done a single productive thing all day. He has not done shit and now he feels like complete shit. He has ice cream for dinner and goes back to the wall. His mind wanders to the mostly blank storyboard, scribbles on Post-it notes and nothing else. He hasn't written anything real in months. He wants something else from the convenience store and feels pangs of remorse.

•

Poise. Poise. Poise. Talking to herself under her breath, Corvus leans against the warm popper and watches the clock. Ten more minutes before the doors close. The theater is dead but there are a few people here for the late show: a young posh couple, an elderly punk couple, and a few lone birds. A customer tells her she should smile more. Corvus imagines bashing his face in as she squirts butter into his popcorn and slides his change to him on the counter. Enjoy the show, she says, still not smiling. Fuck this dude, she thinks.

After the last customer pays and walks off with concessions, Mary runs downstairs from the manager's office red in the face and powers through the glass double doors crying. The door frame shakes a little, and Corvus leans over the counter, watching Mary run through the dark parking lot. Corvus imagines herself shouting after Mary but instead says nothing. Mary disappears into light fog, the surreal orange glow of parking lot lamps.

Dick comes down a few moments later to start closing the theater for the night. He stares out to the parking lot as though he can still see Mary running. When he collects her till, he avoids looking Corvus in the eye and says, Mary and I stopped fucking.

What? Corvus asks. What?

Dick says, You know what.

He knocks the counter with his knuckles, holding the cash till. His voice is cracked and tender. His nose is running.

Let me know when everything's clean, he says. Let me know when the last customer is gone. I'll lock the doors then.

Corvus can see his eyes are red and nods.

When she hears his door lock upstairs, it triggers a sweet feeling: it's her time, closing time. Corvus runs the mop water, doorstops all the doors, and plays Bright Eyes loudly on the stereo tucked under the counter. As though taking a deep dive underwater, Corvus takes a breath and starts sweeping the popcorn into the trash bin, wishing she were back home with Perry. She mouths all the songs echoing in the lobby, wiping down everything spotless. She feels the same but brand-new. Fuck smiling, though. Poise. Poise. Poise. Fuck smiling.

Losing his grip and focus, Perry takes another break from writing his new play and packs a bowl, does a line, and rolls on his back with his arms outstretched. Ten fingers, tall hands outstretched. The city loses daylight through the open blinds of his wall-length window and the floor darkens with stripes. The cool breeze takes him over. He has done absolutely nothing today: complete madness. Absolutely nothing, he thinks. Fucking useless.

Obsessive-compulsive, Perry barely moves and anticipates the time. He knows NPR is airing a review of his play in a few minutes and Perry has everything synced to record. The little red light turns on when the radio announcer's voice comes on air. He takes another quick hit and holds the smoke in, plugging in his headphones and homing in. His eyes seem to open a little wider during the broadcast.

When the segment is through, Perry rewinds the tape and listens again. America hates the play. All the people being interviewed hate the play.

I didn't understand what the BEEP was going on.

REWIND

The little girl disturbed me.

REWIND

No. No, no. Not for me, man. Refund.

Although originally drawing record-breaking crowds during its opening week, audiences are now fleeing from the controversial drama Corvus, *the story of a young girl's suffering.*

Perry takes off his headphones and lights a cigarette and closes his notebook. He is visibly shaking. The tape plays again without him listening, the wheels are spinning. Instead of calling Corvus, he turns his phone off and paces around the studio. He feels blank and hot, anxious and suffocated. Perry sits cross-legged on the floor and dives into his usual stupor: Klonopin, cocaine, weed, a bottle of red wine, and a Diet Coke.

A secret movie geek, Corvus likes never saying a fucking word about it, but she loves being around movies, she loves hearing people talk about movies. She builds her perfect house in the woods in her mind while she sweeps the floor and looks every customer in the eyes while she serves concessions. Corvus kicks open each bathroom stall door to make sure no one is there and nobody's there. Toilets and more toilets. She catches herself in the dirty wall mirror and shakes her head, smiling. The pay sucks, the customers are often rude, but there is a calm here.

There are moments she gets to have to herself that she can't duplicate anywhere else.

The last two people leave the lobby, the older punk couple. Through the glass lobby doors, he has his hand on the small of her back and they're walking in that daze you wander into after seeing a movie. Eyes adjusting, fresh air.

Holding a yellow flashlight, Corvus watches them waddle away before turning off the house lights. She waves at the surveillance camera and calls upstairs.

Dick, I'm doing theater checks, she says.

Do it, says his voice on the phone.

Paradise: The moment when she's alone, when nobody knows what she's doing. The surveillance camera is cheap and only films the main lobby, and Corvus knows all the blind spots. Turning on her flashlight, she unbuttons her uniform and starts to relax. She puts a cigarette in her mouth but doesn't light it. She thinks about Perry and whether he's waiting up for her, as she props open the theater doors.

Little lights illuminate the walking path, a single emergency exit light reaches the high ceiling. After a few paces, Corvus is already walking on top of the seats. She jumps from row to row, armrest to armrest, her favorite kind of special rebellion. Alone with three hundred seats. She does her job and checks for wallets, lost and found things, and to see if anyone is hiding in the empty theater. She feels safe in a space so large, standing on the seats in the front row, looking at the lit blank screen. Corvus makes circles with her flashlight against the walls and seats and takes her time on her way back.

In the last theater, Corvus opens the back exit door and finally lights her cigarette, staring at the orange moon. Fuck, she says.

Corvus knocks on the manager's office door but Dick doesn't seem to be there. She knocks again before she elbows her way in, breaking through the cheap lock. Nothing, no Dick, but the lights are on, the TV is still on.

Walking to the projection booth, she doesn't call for him and walks slowly. There is a figure in the ether, and the projectors are all still running hot. He's sitting in the dark on the old torn couch and he's not moving. Corvus flashes her light over him and asks, What the fuck?

Dick raises a wine bottle to his mouth and takes a swig. He looks up at her and raises the bottle.

No, man, she says, no, thanks, and she sits down next to him, turning on a lamp. Are you doing okay?

Dick looks ahead and takes another swig from the bottle. Underneath the hundreds of movie posters, the walls are paisley. He says, I was closing out and Mary called me, crying. I don't know what to do.

Corvus watches Dick pack his purple bong, which has been hidden in plain sight next to the lamp.

She told me she was hanging out with Louis, Dick says.

Corvus says, Wait. Like hanging out, hanging out?

Yeah. I don't know, Dick says. Yes. His voice breaks when he says yes.

Dick raises the bong to his mouth and inhales smooth thick smoke. He looks up at her and stares at the little distance above her head and raises the bong to her.

Corvus takes the bong and lights the bowl and takes a bigger hit. She coughs just once and cannot help but tear up and smile, eyes tired and dilated.

I can stay here and chill with you if you want.

No, that's okay, Dick says. No worries. He wipes his face with both hands and shakes his head. I can finish closing out if you want to leave.

Corvus stands up and smooths out her jacket. They fistbump and she asks, Are you okay?

Dick nods without looking at her and starts packing another bowl. He turns off the lamplight and breathes in.

When Corvus finally makes her way out to the street, the bars are closing, and the moon looks even bigger and brighter than usual. The sidewalks are filled with people howling at the moon, jumping up and down, and smoking cigarettes. She has to weave in between drunk bodies and conversations, tired as fuck. No one wants to move for her. Corvus lips a new cigarette, looks around, and says, I used to love Saturdays.

Topless women with their faces painted white ride on the shoulders of men dressed as priests on the corner where Corvus waits for her crosswalk light to turn green. Corvus thinks about asking the women, not the priests, what's going on tonight, if there's a party or celebration or something, but instead, she just wonders if they're feeling cold or not.

Before she can get a steady flame from her cheap lighter, Corvus notices a man walking unknowingly into traffic. He looks sad and distracted and moves in this swift motion as though he expects the crowd to follow him across the street. A new row of cars accelerates drunkenly fast across the intersection. Dropping her lighter to the pavement, Corvus screams, Hey, HEY!

The man stops and looks up and sees her. The cars speed by, nearly colliding with him, pulling his jacket with the force of the wind. The look on his face is as pale white as the painted women standing next to Corvus. He looks up again and waves at Corvus and continues walking. He screams, Thank you! and disappears into the flow of people.

Her light turns green and Corvus walks across the street so completely dazed, it takes her an extra twenty minutes to find her route home. She tries to light another cigarette but realizes she forgot to pick up her lighter. When she comes home in the dead of night, she notices right away that Perry's car is not there. In a panic like someone was following her home, Corvus rushes to unlock the front door and runs upstairs, her pulse beating in her ears. Opening the door, looking at the bed: He's not there.

Passed out for hours on the floor, Perry wakes up in a sweat. There are lines and creases on his face and arms: he's dehydrated. It's already the next morning, bright and sunny. He rushes out the door, still putting on his jacket as it slams shut behind him. All his electronics, all the lights in his studio remain on. He worries about Corvus being worried sick and turns on his phone as he races down the stairs.

Perry feels helpless and misunderstood. He wants his body to fall out of time so he can play catch-up or hide inside his mind and shut down. He thinks, There's no time for anything. There's no time for anything.

On the way to his car, Perry runs through the convenience store for something to drink. He has three voicemails waiting for him. The little phone icon pulses like a heartbeat. When he goes to pay, the clerk reaches for his hand. The touch is so soft and gentle, it's startling.

Perry looks up: it's the same young woman with the tattooed cities. No name tag.

She lets go of his hand. She says, I love that record.

What? asks Perry.

She takes the cash he was holding in his frozen fingers and rings up his Diet Coke. The register dings, and she slides him back his old paper receipt. In his handwriting, he reads what he was listening to the other day: Elliott Smith, *New Moon*.

I forgot I gave you this, he says.

I love him, she says. I thought you were listening to him. The clerk takes Perry's hand again and pulls up her sleeve. She points to a skyscraper on her arm, bright red as though raw.

This is the newest one, she says.

Perry nearly reaches out to touch her skin but stops. The clerk smiles for the first time.

She gives him his change and Perry leaves the convenience store; the door sensor chimes and echoes. There is a noticeable breeze and he cannot move. Holding his phone and standing on the corner of the busy street, Perry loses himself and forgets what he was doing. The traffic flows, steady currents of shiny cars and people. The stupid daze leaves his eyes, finally, and he drops the change from his hand, a dime and a few pennies.

CHAPTER 4

THE LAST SCENE IN PERRY'S PLAY COMES IMMEDIATELY
after the intermission: right when the audience has just gotten
comfortable and back to their seats, although some are caught
mid-conversation in the dark, others even still walking back
in. The house goes completely black, dead emergency lights
and everything.

A bright blue light shines on center stage and it's the same
sad girl again. She looks a little older, her dress is ragged, and
her hair is longer. Gigantic white projector screens slowly
tongue down from the ceiling, and an electronic motor is the
only thing heard for a full minute.

Then suddenly images appear, washing the screens and
the girl at center stage: the play happening all over again, playing from the very beginning at 100x speed. The girl looks as
though she is being pummeled by the movies. Dancers with
gauze wrapped around their faces flow from her mind to the

screens and back and forth again, over and over again. The girl fights for her knees not to buckle and her nose begins to bleed, which projects live onto the screens. A close-up.

Corvus and Michelle are sitting close together in the front row. Michelle has her hands gripping tightly on to Corvus's sweater, so automatic.

Then nothing, the movie stops, the whirring motor dies. The screens surrounding the girl are now completely blank. The girl wipes her face with the long sleeves of her wool sweater and finally lies down.

She places the tape recorder on the ground and presses a button.

Perry's voice plays overhead, the blue light goes out:

I keep everything that horrifies me a secret. I pretend that everyone around me is having the worst day of their life. These are etiquettes I practice to weave in and out of the world. I wait in lines in public and lament my past lives. To the woman standing next to me at the bus stop, the lonely cashier at the food co-op, the crowd on the street that pours around me: I imagine you're having the absolute worst day and I won't mess with you. I won't add to your day. I see everyone with the sun in their eyes and I look back at them.

Corvus stretches out in the hallway. She's wearing a new black dress under my sweater that's hers, lying on the floor, full body stretch. The dress is off the shoulder, the floor is wall-to-wall carpet. I have been away and we have been apart and be-

cause we are hard, sad people, I feel fragile when I come into the room. Seeing Corvus brings me immediately home, our inner lives come to life. We shut the blinds. Smoke. Fuck. Smoke. Drink. Fuck. Smoke. Perfect cartwheels in bed. Champagne and serial television.

My usual anger: it opens like a flower and evaporates and vacates. Corvus reaches for me and we go to our desired stupor.

She says, Fuck me numb. The day keeps tearing at me.

With words half in me, I can't quite trace my steps once I get home, and I leave my mind with Corvus. I still wonder. I keep going. I keep going, I keep going.

She whispers in my ear, I admire the way you whittle. All the way down.

The tape recorder clicks off. The screens pull back to the ceiling, the normal house lights click back on. Muscles reawaken, the dream cloud lifts.

The girl, frozen at center stage, doesn't move a beat and her eyes are still shut. The dazed audience, which has dwindled to just a few dozen per showing, watches her and waits for any sign of life. Corvus wonders, How still can she stay? How long can she stay still like that?

It takes a few minutes for the audience to completely give up, as gradually one by one they rise, walk down the narrow aisle, and leave. The house lights buzz above them and Corvus feels like she's in another world, eyes still adjusting to the lights.

Everyone is gone except for Corvus and Michelle and the actor on stage, the beautiful girl with a bloody face.

Corvus walks to center stage; her footsteps tap and faintly echo on the polished wood. Michelle watches her in a daze. Corvus walks tenderly as though approaching an old friend and she suddenly has the shakes. She can't stop shivering. But she keeps walking forward; the draft is so much colder on stage.

The actor gets up, wipes her hands on her dress, and waves at Corvus.

Corvus says, You were so good tonight. She holds her hands together as though praying for a response.

The actor smiles and winks at Corvus.

What I need is a wound and a cold drink, the actor says.

Corvus touches her chest and says, I have a wound.

The actor touches her chest and says, I have a wound too.

Then let's get a drink, says Michelle, jumping onto the stage. She has the biggest smile on her face, already a hundred miles someplace else, wrapping her arms around the necks of Corvus and the actor and leading them down the stairs offstage.

The actor asks, Where is the after-party?

Perry, at the end of the hallway near the front doors, hands a bottle of wine to each woman and kisses Corvus on the side of her eye. He smiles but looks sad, too.

He says, Where is a good question.

CHAPTER 5

BUBBLES RISE TO THE TOP OF THE SPRITZER, AND THE MUSIC gets louder: more bass. Corvus watches the pretty actor walk off with one of the gauze-masked dancers from the play, and she doesn't see her again for the rest of the evening even though, unconsciously, Corvus is still looking for her in the crowd. I never asked for her name, she thinks. More in love with strangers than friends, Corvus looks down at the dance floor: an empty Olympic-size swimming pool, filled with mostly half-naked bodies, awash in fog, perspiration, and more neon flashes. There are DJs spinning where diving boards used to be.

There are more people grinding at the after-party than there were in attendance for Perry's last run of the show. Corvus can see her name, the title of the play, on white vinyl banners along the wall. Directed by Perry.

It means "raven," right?

A man taps Corvus on the back of her shoulder. She turns around and smiles at him, raising her eyebrows ever so slightly. Corvus tilts her head and finds the man handsome.

The man, dressed in an all-black suit, smiles too, and points to the banner.

Corvus? he asks. It means "raven," doesn't it?

It's also a constellation, she says. A fuckload of stars.

And is that a moon? The man smiles again and points at the birthmark on her chest below her collarbone. It has always reminded her of a crescent moon.

He gives her his hand. Corvus takes it and nods.

My name is Tim, he says, and I'm a big fan of your fiancé's. I'm the president of his fan club.

Excuse me? Corvus asks.

My name is Tim, he says.

I'm Corvus, she says.

I know, he says. The lights flicker while they're talking. May I buy you a drink? he asks.

Feeling fresh as death, Corvus loosens and lets go of Tim's hand and waits for him to walk ahead a few paces. Enjoying her distance from him, her dress suddenly feels really good and soft against her skin. It's as though she forgot she was wearing a dress. She can feel the air change around her. She can see a tattoo on the back of his neck as he ascends the stairs. In plain black capital letters, it says MOM.

Corvus leads Tim to Perry, who is waiting in his own

private nook behind a red velvet curtain. Light flashes against the walls and carpet in looping neon patterns. His hand is pressed to the bridge of his wrinkled nose, and he looks stressed out, appearing as though he's having a hard time breathing and sitting still. Something is going on, Corvus notices, something is wrong here. Perry breathes in through the nose, out through the mouth: deep breaths. Corvus thinks, He doesn't look happy at all, and she walks more slowly.

She pats herself for cigarettes, then scans the room for Michelle, rubbing her fingers. The need is a little unbearable, but she finds Michelle in the crowd right away, dancing in the mob. They have this connection, like an invisible string growing taut in the air.

Michelle from the other side of the room has one already in her mouth and is starting to walk outside.

Corvus says, I need a cigarette.

Tim's face lights up and there is a noticeable trace of joy coating his voice when he walks up to Perry and finally manages to say something.

I'm so sorry, he says. My name is Tim. My name is Tim, he says, and I think you're a genius. Absolute genius.

Perry reaches his hand out but doesn't look up.

Thank you, Perry says, eyes still glued to the ground, not even there. I really appreciate that.

They shake hands with varying degrees of strength and effort. Perry really hates shaking hands.

He looks up at Tim and gently says, I hate shaking hands. His eyes are bloodshot, but present and knowing.

Tim says, You've met two of my friends before. Twins. Big men.

I have, yes. Perry looks more meaningfully into Tim's eyes and something new begins, something glows warm. He says, Actually, they've been, like, really nice to me. Like personal bodyguards or something.

Perry pats himself and finds a joint and a lighter.

Are they brothers?

No, Tim answers. They look a lot alike, though.

Where are they now? The tall men.

I think they're dancing in the swimming pool, Tim says. Pretty sure.

Are you the president? Of the fan club?

Yes.

Thank you for supporting my work.

Tim asks, May I please have an autograph?

Perry lights the joint and inhales. His eyes remain closed for what seems to be too long a time and his skin tingles. After blowing out a cloud of thick smoke, he says, I'm sorry, I usually carry a pen, but I don't have one now. Perry doesn't even bother to search his person.

Tim looks up and down and says, I don't think I have one either. It sucks.

Still smoking, Perry says, You can have this, though. He hands Tim a tape recorder.

Tim holds the tape recorder in the palm of his hand like it's made of sharp, precious glass and asks, Don't you use this for everything?

Yes, Perry says, looking down at the floor again. Please go away now.

The club's ceiling is basically a movie screen, and images of big ocean waves in the nighttime play like a film above all the sweaty bodies. Corvus thinks, Lots of water imagery and no water. Everyone is drunk, dazed, and I'm thirsty as fuck. She notices that someone has brought a dog to the party, a big furry baby. She watches the dog from the other side of the bar and pretends to be trapped inside him before going over to hang out with him. She loves this puppy. He's a quiet brown pit bull sitting patiently in the constantly recurring booms of music and other sporadic loud noises. She loves this puppy. She sees some asshole has left him tied to a closed indoor bleacher, but he seems like a good boy.

Hi, baby, Corvus says. She pets him on his stomach as he lies on his back. Collar, but no name tag. She loves the feeling of getting an animal's blessing: a perfect honor.

She leaves the dog to go find Perry, and she can tell by how light her limbs feel that she's a little dehydrated. Every step is a cloud.

She moves a little hair from her eye and says, I see you, Boo.

At the top of the stairs, sitting on the steps hunched over as though entirely sapped of energy, Perry says, Sometimes I feel as though I've forgotten how to have fun.

She touches his face and says, I know. I know you. I love you.

I love you, too, he says. He shivers in this way, something he really only does around her; he feels safe around his Corvus.

Perry has not been feeling safe lately. His talent feels as empty as his stomach. He can only think about the next project, although he has no idea what his next project is yet, which is the problem. His mind spirals.

Corvus tucks her head against Perry's chin and she holds him. He smells like fresh air and nothing. She asks, Did you see that dog down there? Such a beautiful baby!

He's a beautiful boy, Perry says. Yeah.

There is a sadness to the language lovers have. Sleights, tugs, and pulls. There is always something Perry is hiding, something he's not divulging, something he's not saying, but she can read his face. Corvus knows and senses that something is eating him up and his mind is elsewhere but he's looking right at her.

Perry says, I have to stay late tonight. Save face.

She touches his arm and says, Okay. Do you want me to stay with you?

You can go home if you like. I just need to stay here.

She notices that his face seems to droop and darken. She loves his cheekbones. Corvus touches his face and says, I'll see you later, my sweet man. She taps his cheek and he leans his face into her palm and closes his eyes. Perry takes a moment, face in her hand.

Walking downstairs, Corvus looks for the puppy but he's no longer there. The crowd dancing in the swimming pool appears even bigger. Lips a little chapped, she still wants water and heads over to the glowing green exit sign and double doors. Michelle is somewhere in the dark dancing, blowing smoke into the flashing neon lights. Heaven is this place you don't have to be, you're not required, it's really somewhere you're free to do nothing at all, and Michelle swings her head back and takes another pill.

In the cold Corvus makes cloud breaths. As though waiting for her to walk out of the club, Tim is leaning against the wall of the brick building, holding a leash to the happy brown pit bull.

Corvus's face lights up and she goes to pet the dog.

Tim asks, Do you smoke? He shakes a pack of cigarettes.

After waiting for a minute or so, noticing that Perry has not followed right behind her, Tim asks Corvus, Hey. Do you need a ride home? I'm just around the way.

He clears his throat as an ambulance passes by and a few others leave the club, talking, hooting, and laughing loudly. Corvus can barely hear herself as she says, Let's go.

No one knows this secret half-covering my face, Corvus thinks, how anxious I am, how confident I am becoming. There is a degree of mystery she likes to keep in the world, a little unpredictability, and she cannot quite tell what to make of Tim's new, nervous energy. Her natural instinct is to find out more, but she's fucking tired. Being around people fills and drains her but she likes the song and dance.

I like your dog, she says. Her tone is empty, and she just wants to get home.

Corvus chooses a radio station with her boot pressed on the dashboard while Tim speeds toward a freeway entrance. He

drives a fast luxury car and she feels like she's inside a space-
ship. She blindly pets the brown pit bull licking the palm of her
hand from the backseat. She rolls the window down and the air
is freezing but Tim doesn't budge nor lose focus. He casually
looks to the horizon, water shimmering under weak moonlight
farther out from the shore, and says, Hey, I have an idea.

Corvus raises her head.

Let's go down to the water and play with the puppy.

The dog barks.

He takes his eyes off the road for a moment, accelerates
on a dime, makes eye contact with the pit bull, then back to
Corvus.

What do you do? Corvus asks.

He says, I haven't played with him all day.

I'm pretty exhausted, Tim. I think home sounds good.

But before Corvus knows it, her body senses the endless
water and the cold air, and Tim is slowing down and taking the
downhill beach entrance. The road-length rusty gate is open.
It's a public beach but it's after hours: no one else seems to be
around. All the bonfire pits in the near distance are dead and
sandy and the parking lot is empty aside from rocks, sticks,
and detritus. It's cold as fuck outside.

Corvus says, Maybe five, ten minutes, looking at the soft
moonlight on the water.

Come on, boy! Tim screams.

They park half on the grass, and Tim leaves the headlights
turned on, illuminating a small path for them along the sea-
weed, more rocks and white shells. Corvus looks around and

can't believe there is no one else on the beach: the sight is exhilarating, the water looks full of rage.

Are you doing all right? he asks. You look as though you're about to faint.

Like I said, I'm just tired, she says. It would take a lot to make me faint.

Tim hands her a cigarette and they walk side by side, with the puppy leading the way.

Without tact and blowing smoke, Tim asks, So how do you feel about him using your life like that?

Perry's not using me, Corvus says. She shakes her head and smiles.

They're finally down at the water where the sand is dark, but they don't get close enough to get wet. The pit bull waits for no one and quickly splashes into the black waves.

Corvus says, I love his plays. I support Perry.

He portrays you as so sad.

Corvus kind of smiles but stops herself and takes another drag. I *am* sad, she says. So is Perry.

They stop where the moonlight is the brightest and watch the puppy play in the water, each smoking their cigarette, each far gone and exhausted. The clear view of the long, uninhabited shore is a thrilling private celebration that soothes her inside out. The thought of drowning brings goose bumps up and down her arms.

I love the water, she says. She looks at Tim and says, I think Perry makes work for people like me and him. We're just sad people, happy but sad. The wind blows in her hair and she says, Probably our childhood or something.

Before leaving, they walk the dog up a stone path to the cliffs, and take in a more inviting view, the whole stupid Pacific Ocean. As she walks to the edge of the cliff, holding the dog's leash, Tim takes a picture of her without asking first, without her knowing: a girl standing on a cliff, looking out at the water.

He says, My mother is dead. Tossing his cigarette into the grass, he says, We all have fucked-up childhoods. There is this slow gleam in Tim's eyes and he says, That's why I'm a big fan of Perry's. His work is fucked-up good.

He hands Corvus a white business card with just a number on it. XXX-XXX-XXXX.

I would love to work with him in any capacity, Tim says. Or with you, he says.

Tim drives Corvus home and reaches over to open her door.

In any capacity, he says. The beginning of daylight stings her eyes as she walks the last few yards to her red front door, and she can hear insects buzzing secretly all around her and the cold air feels good.

CHAPTER 6

HER WEDDING DRESS IS LACE ON LACE, LIGHT AND SIMPLE with a small bow tied on the back, elegant in its simplicity. Perry is wearing a blue striped suit and a skinny red tie, and he's holding a modest bouquet of daisies. He waits nervously, taking in happy, delighted breaths as though about to fall from the sky. The first look is Corvus coming from around the corner of an old brick building drenched in sunlight after a light rain, and Perry is so surprised, his body temperature changes, and he becomes this perfect steady warmth. His shakes are gone, and they cry softly when they finally embrace. They hold so tightly. There is a new layer to breathing.

They walk into a small room full of photos in square and oval frames: every picture is of strangers, almost all of them smiling. The chapel collects photos of everyone who has ever wed there, displayed as a timeline. There is a smiling officiant named Betty dressed in a white tie waiting for them. There is a jazz piano in the corner, and a couple of rows of wooden benches, and Michelle is sitting in the front, their only invited guest. She looks as though she could explode with everything in her, her smile is the largest in the room. Michelle, excited with her teeth showing, holds her hands clenched in the air as though she's holding invisible ropes.

Even in this perfect moment, Perry feels a tinge of despair just at the tip of his fingers, but he doesn't show it. He looks back and smiles at Michelle, looks at the empty rows of seats behind her, and thinks, The world never wanted us. He thinks, I never believed in family.

Corvus cries reciting her vows and Perry cries while he listens.

Perry cries reciting his vows and Corvus starts to laugh and looks at him, wiping her tears. He smiles looking at her.

They face each other and touch hands. The rings appear. Corvus hops in place after the officiant says, smiling, You may now kiss the bride.

They kiss for a long time, taking a moment for a breath even, as though they won't ever have a chance to touch again.

Corvus holds her veil in her hands, taking a moment to hide her face in Perry's shoulder as Michelle goes to get the car. She softly head-butts Perry's shoulder and says, Hey. Hey, you.

Perry smiles and says, Hey.

Hey, you're mine, she says. You're all mine.

CHAPTER 7

CORVUS WALKS OUT OF THE MOVIE THEATER LOOKING A BIT of a mess; her uniform is wrinkled and spotted with butter stains, but her hair looks really good, and Michelle slow-claps Corvus as she approaches. Her claps grow louder and louder. The parking lot is filled to capacity, four hundred hot cars glowing in the sunshine. The day is insane with lush clouds and stiff winds. They make sweet eye contact, leading to smiles. What the fuck are you doing here? Corvus asks.

Leaning against the Volvo, Michelle pulls out a tightly rolled joint from her pocket with one hand, while snapping chopsticks with the other.

Pure evil genius, Corvus says.

How was work? asks Michelle.

It's the morning shift. It's all dead there.

It's been one week, Michelle says.

Corvus sings, Since you looked at me!

Michelle snorts and says, No! I wanted to surprise you. You've been married for a whole week, asshole!

Michelle offers to drive and lights the joint while starting the ignition, handing it over to Corvus as she leaves the parking lot, ignoring all of her blind spots with complete bliss. Changing lanes, she speeds in total control and inhales. The radio plays Death Grips and Corvus knocks her head back and forth, weaving her hands in the air, tapping the roof of the car as she takes a happy puff. They bounce in their seats, rocking the car along the highway, a little too reckless.

Michelle drives to the rock cliffs overlooking the ocean, where Tim had taken Corvus a few months earlier. Other than being briefly transported back in time, imagining herself standing next to Tim, Corvus doesn't give him another thought as she leaves the car. The wind is even worse here, but the waves are thrilling: all the colors shimmer together.

Michelle says, Married, in a singsong way, holding Corvus's hand. She's carrying a picnic basket.

Corvus smiles and says, Thanks for surprising me with a playdate.

Michelle reaches and gently grabs the back of her neck and says, Babe, I'm always going to be here for you. I know you.

I know you, too, says Corvus, feeling a little faded.

Did you drink at work? asks Michelle.

Corvus snorts through her nostrils and says, Yeah, it was Wow-you're-fucking-married Day. My manager took out his nightly bottle of brandy. And it was dead anyways. Morning shift.

Right on.

The water glitters and glows in the sunset; the waves have a feeling of slowness to them, Corvus thinks.

Michelle gives Corvus a pair of chopsticks and takes out trays of sushi and bottles of beer from the basket. She even takes out a small ice-blue glass bong. I don't have a blanket, but I have this huge-ass sweatshirt, she says.

The ocean turns dark, purple then slowly moving black waves tapping and colliding against the rocky shore. Bits of earth and sand go back and forth in the tide.

I love that sound.

What? asks Michelle.

The water. Listen, Corvus says.

After they finish the beers, the wind gets even more severe and they start to shiver. They take a few rips each from the bong in the cold and Michelle starts laughing maniacally.

What's the craziest thing you've done for love? asks Michelle.

Corvus laughs and snorts again. I got married. How about you?

I ate fucking scrambled eggs with ketchup. This dude, she says.

Corvus continues to laugh and her face can't stop smiling. The black ocean keeps making the sound she loves so much.

Michelle starts screaming, I hate fucking scrambled eggs with ketchup. This dude made me do this. Fuck this dude. What the fuck, ketchup.

It's a thing for people, Corvus says. It's a thing. I've done it myself once or twice.

•

After dropping Michelle off at her place, Corvus nearly falls asleep at the wheel, and pulling up slowly to her street, there are no other cars on the road. For the last few blocks or so, she stops playing music and starts listening to talk radio. In only a few seconds, she feels a wave of dread. The labor of the entire day comes rushing back and she feels as though there are not enough hours in the day, catching the light dying along the horizon. She waits at a red light, almost home, and there is a large crowd of families crossing the street. Corvus tries to look at each individual face but realizes it's impossible. She wonders what kind of family she and Perry will have, if they could handle having children, and the light turns green with people still in the crossing. She feels the long life ahead.

Corvus feels more drunk, stoned, and faded than she has in a long time and she starts to see spots of color. The steering wheel feels smooth and unreal. She presses the garage door remote and speeds a little too quickly into the garage. Corvus hears a sharp snap from the car, and a horrifically crisp yowl. She opens her driver's side door and Pretzel is caught—stuck and very much dead underneath her back wheel, a single stream of blood running downhill toward the garage door. Corvus screams as her garage door starts to automatically close on a timer.

•

Feeling as though the nerves in her arms are pinched, Corvus holds on to the wooden railing of the steps leading into the house. She gets as far as the kitchen, dropping her jacket and keys to the floor, before collapsing into a chair. She is hyperventilating and sobbing. There is some blood on the tips of her fingers from having tried to free Pretzel from the back wheel of the car before she had to stop. Corvus spends a few moments crying with her hands folded against her bouncing lap and taking slow breaths. She walks to the bathroom and washes her hands, splashing her face with cold water. She gets water everywhere but there are no towels in the bathroom for some reason. She walks to the bedroom with her face and hands still wet. Her limbs ache as she guides herself through the dark, not wanting to wake Perry. But he's not there.

The house appears spotless, the floors are mopped and the air is somehow cleaner. No dust. He always does this, she thinks, cleaning without me. The bed is made, and all of their books are organized. Corvus starts breathing normally again, wanting to see and touch Perry. She needs to tell him about Pretzel.

Corvus turns on the lights and opens the door to the basement and walks down. Expecting his voice, she hears nothing but the floorboards creaking under her feet.

At the bottom of the stairs, the bones in her hands immediately chill, as does her skin, as does the blood in her chest. Corvus starts to hyperventilate and shake again. She can see Perry hanging from one of the water pipes along the ceiling, his feet dangling in the air as though levitating, a tight noose wrapped around his neck. Her mouth opens slowly, and everything falls down a hole, everything, everything she has goes down a cold hole. She doesn't remember screaming as she falls to her knees. Her teeth and gums hurt as she spies a note a few feet away: *I'm so sorry, baby.* A few words are scratched out in pen. His pale bloody wrists are wrapped in towels.

CHAPTER 8

AFTER THE FUNERAL, CORVUS DISCOVERS THAT HER BODY can move on its own. She can move from room to room, building to building, function to function, without much thought or feeling. There is a fog that takes over. Letters and bills have been piling up in her mailbox, which she has stopped checking: past-due notices, growing debt, and colorful advertisements. She answers the door and the phone but can barely recall any of it. Words and faces and condolences all wash over her. Gravity pulls.

She has not heard from Michelle for weeks and Michelle did not attend the funeral, but Corvus remembers a bouquet of daisies with a card simply signed *Michelle.*

Corvus has stopped going to the movie theater and Dick has stopped calling. Louis and Mary have stopped calling.

The biggest event of her week for the past month has been

going to the store for cigarettes and simple groceries: potato chips, peanut butter, bread, toilet paper. Her appetite wanes and turns into the need for sleep. The bed—their old bed—is this deep, precious space, the only thing she wants. She listens to whatever tape recordings she has of Perry, never changing her clothes, never wanting to leave the small comfort of their old sheets, her few yards of sanctuary.

When Michelle finally reaches out, it's six months after Perry's death and Corvus notices it's a beautiful sunny day as she opens the front door and somehow makes tea and coffee for the two of them.

Michelle says, I can't be a friend to you right now. I just can't. She is wearing a tight dress and a flashy leather jacket as though ready for a long night out on the town, which, for the first time in their relationship, disturbs Corvus. On the other side of the patio table, Corvus is wearing Perry's old sweater and feels a sinkhole in her chest.

Michelle lights a cigarette for Corvus and finishes the last of her coffee before rushing off.

Corvus remembers a kiss on her cheek, and a gentle hand rubbing her neck, and never sees Michelle again. That's really it. The sensation of touch barely registers. Her cigarette ashes over. The open front door brings a draft into the room but she doesn't bother to close it.

Some slights change your life. Some betrayals knock you so deeply out of sync that you question how you can ever recover. Corvus decides Michelle is simply dead to her. You're fucking dead to me, Corvus thinks. If Michelle ever comes up in conversation, she is simply dead. The door is closed, the book is shut, the fire burning the bridge will burn forever.

Corvus says, Okay, okay.

A foggy, wasted year passes after Perry's funeral. One afternoon, Corvus finds Tim's wrinkled business card in her pocket. After a single ring, Tim picks up and things go foggy again. It is as though he knew she was going to call and there is no emotion in his voice. There is no point in feeling, she thinks. Returning the same void of emotion, Corvus says, Okay, okay. He offers her a plane ticket and a job. She smokes her last joint in the house with the patio doors open and packs her backpack sparingly, occasionally taking a moment to cry in Perry's old basement. Her brain feels soft, her nose runs and runs.

Although she's slept most of the day, most of the week, Corvus feels so tired she can no longer feel her feet on the ground.

XXX-XXX-XXXX.

Corvus waits for her bus to the airport at the transit station. The sunshine stings her eyes before it starts to feel good again. The warmth spreads to her cold face, to what coalesces into a face. The hunger she feels is unlike any hunger she has ever felt. She walks over to the McDonald's next to the transit station and orders a number one.

She feels a tap from behind her, and when she turns around, it's a deranged woman standing there, possibly homeless, dressed in a tattered sweater and worn old jeans. The woman looks at Corvus with bloodshot eyes and points at her with shaking hands.

She says, I was hit by a car this morning. I was hit by a car this morning.

Not knowing what to say, Corvus takes the woman's hand in her hand and they wait in line together. Corvus says, I was hit by a car too. This makes the woman smile and she embraces Corvus. The woman smells like urine and she starts to tap Corvus on the shoulder again. The woman points off in the distance, toward the glass double doors, and Corvus can see that there is nothing there. Only the transit station.

The woman says, There is a man out there talking to me. Like he knows me.

She goes on, I was hit by a car this morning. Her eyes get more bloodshot as she lets go of Corvus. She leaves the Mc-Donald's right as her order number is called.

PART THREE

ALL GOLD EVERYTHING

CHAPTER 1

IT STARTS WITH A JOLT: AN ELECTRIC FENCE VIBRATES. Corvus wakes up sore and parched on a straw bed, locked inside a metal dog kennel. The dark room smells like wet dog, barely illuminated by a hanging ceiling light. She feels as though she hasn't seen light in days, and her eyes squint shapes into view. There are roaming pit bulls in one cage, Corvus and Amber in the other. Looking up from the cracked concrete floor, she can see a sign posted on the wall with a lightning bolt and a sad face. Corvus hears her own voice inside her head: don't touch the cage door.

Trapped inside the same rusty cage, Amber is still out cold. She has a raw wound on the back of her head, but the bleeding has stopped. Corvus kisses Amber's unconscious face and raises her arm from the straw bed: they are bound together with gold handcuffs.

Amber? she asks. Amber?

Corvus gently taps her cheek to try to wake her. She turns around and breathes in and assesses the room.

Through the metal cage door, the dogs have started barking. They bark but keep their distance from the electric fence. Marco is the only dog roaming free, not in either cage. When he sees Corvus, he starts to whimper. He's smart enough to come only close enough to not get shocked by the fence. She can see the very sad look on his face. He wants to be closer.

She says, Marco. With a deep fear in her voice, she says, Good boy, Marco.

Behind the loyal animal, there is a table set not too far away. Fine linen, unlit tall candles, and shiny china. A door opens upstairs and Corvus pauses. Hearing footsteps descend, she quickly collapses back on the straw bed and pretends to be asleep. Marco, not giving her away, goes to the stairs and, despite the other dogs' constant barking, does not make a sound.

Camila and Tim appear, holding hot plates: roasted chicken, mussels, and whole lobsters. Camila even has a bottle of champagne. Through her closed eyelids, Corvus notices they don't even appear to look her way. She breathes very slowly through her nostrils and acts like a stone.

Hug me, Camila demands.

Tim does. He sits down, scoots his chair in, and places a napkin on his lap. He pulls a greasy leg off the chicken and starts eating right away.

Camila goes to the back wall and takes out a large saber from a chest, its sharp blade longer than her arm, and removes the leather sheath swiftly and smoothly like a dance. The sight nearly causes Corvus to utter a sound, but she stays calm. Her breathing skips back to normal.

To the start of a new fiscal year, Camila says. Her smile is calculated. She looks eager for the future.

Tim says, Hear, hear, his mouth still greasy, taking no pause from the chicken. He looks bored. Marco wags his tail, sitting patiently next to the two of them.

Camila slides the blade up against the neck of the bottle and slices off the cork: POP!

They pour what champagne doesn't get onto the floor into their thin glasses. They clink their glasses together, drink, and proceed to eat the entire meal without saying another word to each other. Camila, by far, eats more than Tim, taking her time cracking open each and every lobster. She sucks the meat from the shell and looks to be in another place.

Tim asks, Did you transfer more money into my account?

This morning, she says. More than you asked for. Should last you the better part of the year.

Her eyes look bloodshot. Camila says, I want one hundred films. I want one hundred sixty-minute films by the end of the year. She claps her hands once, and the dogs stop barking. Camila turns to look at Corvus, who is still pretending to be dead asleep in the cage.

I want to expand, Camila says. I want another island.

Tim says, I just want a little revenge. He uses his bare hands as a napkin to wipe his mouth and touches the new scar on the back of his head.

Camila says, Whatever. I don't care, as long as I get one hundred films. They're already yours.

Camila burps into her napkin and smiles as though pleased with herself. She waves her hands like a fan at her face.

Breaking his discipline, Marco starts to whimper at the remains of the food.

I'm going to let him out, Tim says. He leads Marco upstairs and shuts the door before returning.

Tim stands next to Camila and picks up the empty champagne bottle.

This is good, he says. He taps the label.

It's my favorite, she says.

Mind the glass, Tim says. He swings the bottle against the back of Camila's head and she falls to the concrete floor, her chair and the table toppling down with her as the dishes break. The dogs locked inside the kennel start barking again, now even more loudly, and Corvus jolts slightly, lying there with her eyes still closed, trying not to give herself away.

Tim spins and catches the champagne bottle in the air. He says, Huh, it didn't break.

He goes over to the wall and turns off the electricity and comes closer to Corvus's cage. All the dogs continue to bark, some of them jumping against the metal fence now that the electricity has been turned off, all of them snarling and showing teeth.

Tim stands there for a long time while the dogs bark.

He kicks the fence with his shoe. He kicks it again.

Are you awake? he asks.

Are you awake?

CHAPTER 2

IN BROAD DAYLIGHT, TIM PREPS A SMALL BOAT ON THE shore of the island. Pebbles and white sand get stuck to his shoes and shins. The water is blue, clear, and calm. He removes Amber's and Corvus's handcuffs, but Corvus still does not move, never giving herself away. She looks dead to the world and her mask does not waver. He carries them up the stairs to the boat, Amber first, then Corvus, while Marco paces the shore with his tongue hanging out. The boat is cold and wet from the morning dew. It rocks gently back and forth as Corvus lets in more light through her eyes. Tim looks annoyed but resolute, as though performing a simple household chore.

Around the lake, the ravens talk in the trees.

Corvus looks through her eyelashes as though looking through a pinhole angled toward hell. This day will not kill her, she thinks. Clenching her teeth, in the black of her eyes, in the back of her mind, she repeats in her head, This day will not kill me.

Tim looks back at the mansion and the clouds overhead and starts the motor. He unties the boat from the dock and Marco jumps into the hull as Tim speeds off.

Marco starts to lick Corvus's face, but still she does not budge. Marco whimpers and goes over to Amber and begins almost desperately licking her face. The boat cuts through the water, the sunlight reflects in the spray on all sides. The motor hums and Corvus can feel the vibrations through the hull of the boat.

Amber starts to shiver and her face spasms. The life appears back in her face and her eyes open, her chest rises up and down.

Marco runs over to the side of the boat and barks and barks. He can see the pod of hippos splashing in the shallow water just on the shore. Valerie is rocking his head violently up and down before he starts to run on the sand toward the water. The pit bull is the only one that notices Valerie, and he barks like his whole body is being torn apart from the inside. The motor is louder than his bark but he keeps barking. The dog knows what blind rage nature is bringing.

Tim holds the saber in his hand and says, Good morning. He shakes the saber at Amber. Do not move, he says. Or move and see what happens.

Amber rubs her face with her hands and licks her lips. My head, she says, wincing in pain. What the fuck is going on?

Corvus can see something in the water. She watches Marco

furiously barking and looks back toward the mansion and the island. More and more hippos dive into the water.

Valerie hears the sound of the terrible motor from the boat and pops over the net and the buoys. The net splinters apart in the water, the buoys separate and knock against one another. Valerie moves like a demon in the water.

Tim looks straight ahead then back down to Amber and Marco, completely unaware of anything happening beneath the water. Valerie's head resurfaces a few yards from the boat, popping up to take a breath, eyes mad with frenzy and a sharp black color. Blood sweat. This is his lake, and he wants the boat.

Marco barks at the charging hippo, but Tim does not turn around, still pointing his saber at Amber. His other hand guides the boat's steering wheel, and Corvus can finally see the hippo approaching, a rising bulge in the water.

Marco barks and jumps to bite Tim's hand, sinking his teeth into his flesh, as Tim screams in pain.

Corvus rises and grabs the saber. She punches Tim in his neck, as Marco keeps his bite and holds on to Tim's right hand.

Valerie lunges out of the lake toward the boat, exposing his entire gigantic body, and collides with the motor. The boat miraculously does not smash to pieces, nor does it flip over, but everyone falls into the lake: Corvus, Amber, Tim, even Marco.

Rising to the surface, Corvus can smell a strong sulfurous smell, like rotten eggs.

Valerie, with his large canine tusks and sharp incisors, lunges again from under the lake, grabbing hold of Tim's midsection. Tim screams into the sky. Corvus goes down and resurfaces from a close but safer distance. She can see the wiry bristles on the hippo's snout. Blood rises in clouds from Tim's body. Valerie shakes him like a rag doll, dragging him back down under the water again and again, crushing whatever he has of Tim in his mouth into a pulp. Tim's organs become visible, his lungs a dark, deep red, floating from his body in the cold water.

Corvus and Amber swim madly until they reach the boat. Amber screams like bloody murder, unharmed but wet and shell-shocked. These eyes have seen something new. Corvus reaches to pull Marco into the boat, and she kisses the dog on his head. With the motor disengaged, Corvus grabs the oars on either side of the boat and starts to row through the water with every muscle in her body. Her limbs and joints hurt as though being torn from the inside out, and even her eyes burn. After a few seconds, Amber takes one of the oars and helps her row, constantly turning her head back toward the clouds of blood in the water. Marco barks, but Valerie does not seem to be following the slow-moving boat. The hippo is still busy, dragging Tim's body, shaking him over and over again.

CHAPTER 3

WHEN THEY REACH THE OTHER SHORE, IT'S AS THOUGH they have never been on land before, it's so beautiful to touch sand. The trees tower over them, perfect, fresh air. The ravens continue to talk. Corvus takes Amber's pale hand as they limp to their parked car, still there, with the keys resting in the glove compartment, still there. Marco follows them with his tail wagging as though it's just another day in the woods. The light peeks through the tree branches and the fog. The radio starts with the ignition and Corvus breathes in deeply as though just getting out of the water. She leans her chair back in the driver's seat, all the way back it can go, and reaches for the ceiling of the car, with her body feeling like jelly and nothing. Amber touches her hair and taps Corvus's arm.

Are you okay? Amber asks. Are you good?

The radio plays another Robyn song as they hold eye contact with each other. Hearing the song makes them laugh hysterically until their stomachs hurt and burn. A pop song. Then they weep together, as though melting into each other. Tears and sweat and blood and runny noses. Corvus breathes in deeply again, adjusting her seat back upright. Marco barks.

I am so good, Corvus says. So good, she says, shaking. She can hardly feel her thumbs.

She feels the stillness of the highway as they approach it, the light flowing into her eyes. There is something invisible fueling strength into the tight grip of her hands, turning the leather steering wheel and magically accelerating the car.

THANK YOU

My deepest thanks and eternal gratitude to Yuka Igarashi for loving this book and for taking me on. You changed my life.

My deepest thanks and eternal gratitude to Allie Wuest, my incredible editor and kindred spirit. You are the greatest of all time.

Thank you so much to everyone at Soft Skull.

Thank you to my dear friends who have provided me comfort and support while writing this book: Thom Crowley, Tara Atkinson, Willie Fitzgerald, Rebecca Brown, Christine Texeira, Molly Woolbright, Kristen Steenbeeke, Matthew Simmons, Stephen Danos, Matt Nelson, Peter Mountford, Anastacia Renee, Sonora Jha, Chelsea Martin, and Ana Carrete. I am thrilled by all of you.

Thank you to Patty and Ron, Edith and Rauan, Rachel, Meggie and Michael, Sarah and Jake, Hannah and Spencer, and Jeremy.

Thank you to others who unknowingly provided words and phrases and ideas for use in the writing of this novel: Thalia Field, Ciara, Robyn, Josephine Foster, and Tegan and Sara.

Thank you to Adam Robinson, Blake Butler, and Chelsea Jean Werner-Jatzke for publishing excerpts from *King of Joy*.

Thank you so much to my best friend, Frances Dinger.